BILL*Dirty*ONAIRE

Book One of the Dirty Billionaire Trilogy

MEGHAN

MARCH

Visit my website at www.meghanmarch.com

ABOUT DIRTY BILLIONAIRE

I've got a big... ego and an even bigger bank account. That's pretty much where my bio ends. Honestly, I don't need to say anything else. I've just sold 99% of women on going home with me. Do I sound like a jerk to you? That's because I am. And guess what? It works for me just fine. Or at least it did. Until I met her. Books talk about sparks flying. Screw that. With her, it was like emergency flares mixed with jet fuel. Or maybe just straight up napalm. Only one problem. She wouldn't tell me her name or her number when she disappeared from the hotel room after the hottest night of my life. Now I've had a taste of the perfect woman and I need it again. So what's a jerk to do? I took this problem to the street. A missed connection gone viral. And when I find her? I'm keeping her.

Dirty Billionaire is the first book in the Dirty Billionaire Trilogy. Creighton and Holly's story continues in *Dirty Pleasures* and concludes in *Dirty Together.*

For those who dream so big, they scare themselves. Don't ever stop.

CHAPTER
ONE

HOLLY

Country Star JC Hughes Caught Between a Cock and a Hard Place

How is he going to explain this one away to girlfriend Holly Wix and his fans?

"That two-timin' son of a . . ."

I hiss under my breath as I stare at the headline—and the compromising picture accompanying it—splashed in vivid color across the front page of the gossip rag displayed prominently in the checkout line at my supermarket. For the second time in two months, it's a picture of my "boyfriend" locked in an unmistakably passionate embrace with another woman, except this time she's wearing a giant black strap-on.

The edges of the paper crumple in my sweaty grip, and I fight the urge to tear it to shreds, along with every copy sitting on the rack in front of me.

He's going to destroy my career before it even has a chance to become a reality.

One year, they said. One year in this joke of a "relationship" and I'd earn my stripes, be all set in the world of country music. Judge me all you want for agreeing, but when your brand-new record label puts something like that in the contract that will jet you out of the backwoods town you're dying to escape, you don't ask questions. You sign on the dotted line.

But reality is a cold slap in the face, and some days it hits you when you're standing in line at the grocery store. What happens when they finally catch JC with a guy? His habit of swinging both ways, but preferring men to women, is about to become the worst-kept secret in Nashville.

I'm Holly Wix, winner of a make-me-a-star TV show, and handpicked by the label to buoy JC's once-impressive but now flagging career. It didn't seem like a big deal when they slipped it into my contract in the beginning. What starry-eyed girl wouldn't be thrilled to have her name linked to a country star?

Instead of the one-way ticket to stardom I naively expected, I'm becoming the butt of every industry joke faster than the guys back home can spend their paycheck on twelve-packs and scratch-offs. But I've got one shot at keeping this dream career alive, and honestly, there's nothing I wouldn't do to save it. So this situation with JC needs to get settled before things spiral further out of control.

Tugging the bill of my trucker hat lower, I glance around to see if anyone has noticed me flipping out in the checkout line. A woman behind me clucks her tongue as she pulls her sunglasses out of her baby's mouth.

Crap.

That cluck of her tongue was aimed at me, not the toothless, blue-eyed, smiling baby. Surprisingly, though, the expression on her face is sympathetic, not angry.

"Men are assholes, am I right? Being famous just makes them bigger ones."

I smile weakly, and she continues. "Don't believe everything you read in the papers, doll. They're always ninety-five percent bullshit. Probably Photoshopped. He should have his head examined if he's cheating on you."

Snapping my gaze back to her, I read recognition all over her face, despite my hat, glasses, complete lack of makeup, and relatively low level of fame. I force a smile onto my face, but it feels awkward and fake.

"It's called a gossip rag for a reason, I guess?" I reply, failing at my attempt to inject some humor into my tone.

She nods and gestures to the half dozen bottles of wine in her cart. "This probably sounds crazy forward, but you look like you could use a drink and someone to vent to."

Vent to a perfect stranger I met in the grocery store? That would be insane, not to mention dangerous. If I did, the "she said" side of the story would be splashed all over tomorrow's papers, and the label would kill me—the painful death of breach of contract and being blackballed in the industry.

I already used up strike one the first time a picture of JC hit the papers. I marched right into Homegrown Records' offices and told them their devil's deal wasn't worth it, and that I wouldn't help JC's career at the expense of my own.

Their response? If I didn't turn around, march my ass right back out of the office, and paste a smile on my face, they'd yank me off my tour, and I'd be a has-been before I ever got the chance to become a someone.

I'd go to bat for my career any day of the week, but faced with the threat of losing it, I'm ashamed to say I backed down and toed the company line. You only get one shot at your dream. It's not something I'm willing to let go . . . regardless of how much of my pride I might have to swallow. Which brings me back to the gossip rag and the woman in front of me.

An awkward silence stretches between us in the checkout line as all the scenarios swirl through my brain of how I can reply to her. Finally, she smiles, and there's something kind and knowing in her expression.

"I know what you're thinking—you can't spill your side of the story to anyone. Too risky." She lifts her hand and flashes a giant rock on her left ring finger. "But I'm not just anyone. I've been on the front page of the tabloids too, and I know exactly how much it sucks. After being married for a decade to the biggest reformed horndog of them all, I'm no stranger to any of it. On top of that, I'd never break the vows of sisterhood."

My gaze darts from the giant diamond to her face. Studying her makeup-free features, it finally hits me. "You're Tana Vines."

Tana Vines was the Female Country Artist of the Year about ten years back, and her husband was awarded Entertainer of the Year at least four or five times during that time. They're country music legends. A true power couple.

She holds out her hand and I shake it, operating purely on instinct.

"Yes, I am," she says. "It's nice to meet you, Holly Wix."

Two bottles of wine later, Tana and I lay sprawled on chaise lounges beside her indoor pool. Behind the gated walls, and in the presence of someone I listened to on the radio in junior high, I finally have a chance to unburden all the crap that has been filling my head for months.

"Six more months? That's a hell of a long time to put up with JC's bullshit. Not to mention keeping your own legs closed. Good Lord, girl. Aren't you dying to get some dick?" Tana asked.

An embarrassed laugh escapes my lips. "Um, I've been pretty preoccupied with learning the ropes, I guess."

"Well, shit. I'd be dying for dick."

I shake my head. "I don't want to do anything to jeopardize my position with the label. I have a feeling that if my picture ended up in the paper the way JC's has, the double standards would have me out on my butt so fast, I couldn't even yell 'Bingo!' first."

Tana rolls onto her side and faces me. "That's probably the truth, but it don't make it fair. The only reason they're covering his ass is the shelf of awards he's got from five years ago, and all the money they've got invested in him. You're the perfect image booster. But you're right—you're expendable if you step out of line."

I already looked up to Tana as a country idol, but now I have to say I have a bit of a girl crush. She doesn't sugarcoat anything, and it's refreshing in this world of people who say one thing and mean something completely different.

"Who's expendable?"

A deep voice echoes through the pool room as Mick Vines walks in. The man—a living country legend—picks up one of the empty bottles on the table between our lounge chairs. "And damn, Tana. I've been lookin' for you for a half hour."

"Gemma knew where I was." Gemma, I learned, was Tana and Mick's live-in nanny.

Tana sits up as Mick sets the bottle down and leans over to press a kiss to her lips.

"There. Been lookin' for that. My little bit a sugar."

I turn my head away as Tana wraps her hand around the back of his neck and pulls him in for another kiss, this one not nearly so innocent. She doesn't seem to care that I'm intruding on their intimate moment. And it's a moment that makes me wish even more that I wasn't trapped in this mess.

Not that I'm looking for what they have—because I'm truly not. I'm not looking for that kind of happily-ever-after for a good five or ten years. I'm too young for that, and my focus is on my career, exactly where it's supposed to be when you're standing on the edge of achieving the dream you've had since you were ten years old.

But even on that edge, I'm still only a puppet with the label pulling the strings. Six months in, and I'm already sick and tired of being yanked in the directions they want me to go. What could I accomplish if only I could cut those tethers and come into my own? But slicing those ties would mean sacrificing what I've already accomplished, and that's not an option.

Mick stands tall again and notices me for the first time. "Who's our guest, babe?"

It's much less of a surprise that he doesn't recognize me than it was for Tana to make the connection. Honestly, I'm still a nobody in this industry. I'm working my tail off on becoming a somebody, and I've got fans, but to someone at Mick Vines's level, I'll always be a nobody.

I smile and hold out my hand. "Holly Wix."

His eyes narrow as he shakes my outstretched hand. "I've heard your name. Why have I heard your name?"

I'm stunned that there's even a hint of recognition in him. My stomach turns in big flopping waves, and Tana jumps in, saving me from bumbling whatever explanation is about to fall from my lips.

"I picked up Holly in the checkout line while we bonded over how much it blows to see yourself on the front of a gossip rag."

Mick's gaze narrows further before it lights with knowledge. "Wix. You're the hot young thing JC Hughes has on his arm these days."

I cringe at the description, because that's not how I want to be known. *But that's what happens when you sign a deal with the devil.*

Tana slaps his thigh from her seated position. "And she's touring with Boone Thrasher because she's the hottest new talent to hit the stage since Carrie and Miranda."

7

Her adamant statement throws me for a loop, and those nervous waves in my belly glimmer with pride.

Mick rocks back on the heels of his tooled black leather boots. "Ain't heard her sing yet, but I've sure seen her picture."

I wince, pride doused.

"And that's the problem. The label has backed her into a corner, and they've made the JC situation a requirement. She can't get out of it," Tana explains.

Mick studies me. "Who you with, girl?"

"Homegrown. They signed me when I won *Country Dreams*."

"Ah." Mick nods twice. "Now I know where I first heard your name. And you probably signed a devil's bargain to get your 'million-dollar recording contract' after you won."

It isn't even a question. Mick knows how the game is played.

"It was that or keep working at a bowling alley in BFE, Kentucky, and never taking my shot. At least this got me to Nashville."

He raises a hand. "No need to get defensive. I'm not judging. We all take the route we need to take to get here, but that means living with the consequences. How long are you stuck with this JC bullshit? I'm assuming you have to suck it up and smile on his arm to help shine up his image and get some good press. Besides, we all know he's been on the edge of casino-playing retirement for a more than a few years now."

Dang. Mick really does know how the game is played.

I guess you couldn't be in Nashville as long as he has without learning all the pitfalls.

"Six months," Tana offers. "And it's not like when our managers hooked us up. JC doesn't seem to care either way if he hurts Holly's career."

I swivel my head around to stare at Tana. "I didn't know that you . . ." I glance back to Mick. "Really? Your relationship started out as a publicity stunt?"

Tana laughs. "Of course it did. Why else do you think I'd get involved with such a man-whore? I needed some street cred, and he was getting all the wrong kinds of press for sleeping with everything with tits."

"Jesus, baby. That's ancient history—and we kept that shit quiet for a reason."

"I'm just saying that sometimes it actually works out fine," Tana says.

Mick shakes his head. "Back to the point of this conversation." Aiming his stare at me, he continues. "You could be fucked in six months if JC keeps this shit up. You've got sympathy on your side right now, but if you keep laying down and taking it, you're just going to look like a fool."

Tana slaps his thigh again. "Not helping."

Her husband reaches down and grabs her hand. "Quit, woman, or I'll spank your ass even harder tonight."

Tana's face flushes a bright red, and I decide to let the comment go without trying to figure out exactly what they're talking about.

Mick releases her hand and grabs the magazine shoved between the wine bottles. "This the rag with the cheating dick?"

Shaking her head, Tana grabs it from his hand. "Nope, that's the one with the hot billionaire dick I'm going to marry if you decide to leave me for some country starlet."

I catch a glimpse of the cover. It's a copy of *Forbes*, and there's a stupidly handsome dark-haired man on the cover.

The headline reads: CREIGHTON KARAS CRUSHES COMPETITION.

"What are you talking about, woman? You'd bury me out back if I so much as looked at another woman," Mick grumbles.

Tana's lyrical laugh echoes off the walls. "Damn right, and don't you forget it."

I snatch the magazine out of his hand to get a closer look.

"Whoa, girl. Calm down."

I wave him off, the wine dulling the instincts that would otherwise have me continuing to bow and scrape in his country-music royalty presence.

"Shhh. I need to look at him." I'm not sure why I need silence to do that, but apparently the large bottle of wine I drank says I do.

The man is gorgeous, but he looks cocky and arrogant. I flip the magazine open and page through it until I find another picture of him.

I win because losing isn't an option.
—Creighton Karas

I know I'm truly drunk when the only thought filtering through my brain is how much I'd like to be his prize when he's winning. *Where the hell did that come from?* And like I'd even know what to do with a man like that. He's so far out of my league, it's not even funny.

I glance over at Mick and Tana, who are once again locked in a tangle of lips and limbs.

And . . . that's my cue to leave.

I slap the magazine shut and rise on shaky legs. "I should probably get going."

Tana pulls away from Mick and raises an eyebrow in my direction. "Honey, you ain't driving anywhere. I'll go make up a guest room. It's the very least I can do since I got you shitfaced."

"Not necessary. I should get home. I have . . . a plant that needs water. Or something."

I squint because I can't remember if my plant is dead or alive. I haven't watered it in as long as I can remember. Apparently I'm thinking too hard about plants, which might be alive or dead, and not concentrating on my balance because I tip forward.

Mick catches me with an outstretched palm. "Come on, honey. We're putting you up tonight. Won't hear anything different."

He turns me around and marches me toward the door that leads into the sprawling mansion. "Besides, it seems like someone needs to take you under their wing so you don't get chewed up and spit out by this bitch of an industry. My wife isn't exactly the type to bring home strays, so she must've seen something in you needing a little protection. We're gonna make sure you have it."

My eyes burn, and I blink back the unexpected tears. I've been in this town for six months, essentially friendless, and in one night I've apparently been adopted by two people I never thought I would ever have a chance to meet.

"G'night, Holly. I'll see you in the morning, sweets," Tana calls from behind me.

Apart from those blissful moments standing onstage, for the first time in months I have a genuine smile on my face, and I feel like I belong somewhere.

It doesn't last long.

CHAPTER TWO

HOLLY

"We'll put your ass on a bus back to Podunk if you don't toe the line, Wix. That bowling alley you used to sing at? They won't even let you back onstage when I'm done tearing you apart," Morty, the jerk-off record exec, rails at me in the conference room of Homegrown Records.

It's been two months since the night I met Tana, and JC has managed to land in the paper three more times. I can't let this stand any longer. I've officially become the laughingstock of Nashville, and I can't take any more pitying looks from the guys on my tour.

When the bus pulled into town this morning, I went directly to Tana's house first. We've kept in touch, and every time I've been back in town on a break, she's made time to get together. It's the first real friendship I've had since Mary Jane Devo married her Marine sweetheart and moved to Hawaii almost two years ago.

I'm not the kind of girl who makes friends easily—mostly because I work as much as I can, and I never have extra money to go shopping or get a pedicure. But now when it matters, and I'm living in a new town and knee-deep in a business where I'm not sure who I can trust, Tana has been a lifesaver.

Her advice was to tell them to fuck off and take my chances. So this morning I grew a pair of lady balls and marched into the office to tell them to screw this JC nonsense because it isn't worth it.

I just didn't plan on JC being there too.

"What the hell do you have to complain about?" he says, leaning back in the cushy leather conference room chair. "You're getting plenty of press. Maybe you're still too green to realize it, but there ain't no such thing as bad publicity."

I want to smack the smug look off JC's face. He's baiting me, just waiting to see if I'll push Morty any further and get myself thrown back on that bus to Podunk.

"Well, in this case, I think you're wrong," I say, holding my chin high. "Crushing my career doesn't seem like good business."

JC laughs. "You're just gettin' started, sweetheart. This is the best thing that ever happened to you. I guess I can try to be a little more discreet . . . ," he says, glancing at Morty.

Morty nods. "Good, then we're done here."

Oh no. No, we are not done here.

"I don't think so," I say, and point at JC. "He needs a babysitter to keep it in his pants, not a pretend girlfriend. If you want to save his career, why don't you focus on putting out more hits, not on his love life?"

"I love when you talk about me like I'm not even here, baby," JC drawls. "Maybe I'll write a love song for you. How'd ya like that?"

He was patronizing me. I've never been exactly sure what that word means, but I'm pretty sure this is it.

"Don't call me—" I start.

"Girl, if you don't—" Morty interrupts, most likely to threaten me some more, but Jim, his partner, jumps to his feet and presses both hands to the solid wood surface of the conference room table.

We both shut up and look his way.

"You know, I think we're going about this all the wrong way," Jim says, nodding and looking very much like a man with a plan.

Relief filters through me at the hope that Jim might be seeing some sense. But my hope and relief are doused just as quickly as he continues.

"I don't think it's less of a relationship that we need for you two, but more."

What in the world? More?

I look at JC, but he looks puzzled too.

"Go on," he says. "I can't wait to hear this idea."

I'm pretty sure I could wait the rest of my life and never hear this idea and be perfectly happy. This is probably the moment I should march out of the room and search for some time rewinding device, because I have a feeling things are about to go from bad to worse for me.

Jim looks from JC to me and then back to Morty, his eyes lighting with excitement. "JC and Holly will get engaged; it'll be perfect. We can set it up so it's all public."

He pauses and rubs his hands together like a kid on

Christmas morning. "New Year's Eve. That's it. Boone and Holly's tour will be on break, and JC, we got you that spot on *Dick Clark's New Year's Rockin' Eve*. You can propose at midnight, and it'll be fucking brilliant PR."

As my chest tightens in horror, Jim looks at me. "The press will forget about all this bullshit in the papers because they love a good celebrity romance. JC will put out a statement about how he's been sorting through some things, but now he has his priorities in line and he's ready to move forward."

No, this is not happening.

"What?"

My voice, which is capable of hitting some pretty earsplitting high notes when necessary, screeches through the conference room, and for a moment I hope I have the vocal capacity to shatter the glass door.

I don't.

I look at JC, who has slapped his hands over his ears. "Whoa, girl. Easy on the ears."

"You can't agree to this!" I yell. "This is insane!"

Morty slaps the table. "Jesus fucking Christ, Wix. Calm the hell down. It's not like you have to marry the man. Just pretend to be engaged for four months. Maybe longer, depending on how things go."

I bite my lip until the coppery tang of blood fills my mouth. It's the only way I can stop myself from screaming and cursing them out. And maybe, you know, murdering them. I'm from the backwoods; I know how to hide bodies.

One phrase repeats in my head: *Maybe longer?*

Four months. That's what's left of my contract. Four.

Months. And then Homegrown won't own my soul. Oh, they could still try to blackball me, but they won't have a legal hold over me.

I can't do this. JC will never agree, either. Right?

I walk around the table to JC and sit down next to him. "You can't think this is a good idea. You can't go along with this."

JC just smiles his easy good-ole-boy smile and lays his hand over mine. "You ever worn a strap-on before, baby? Because I think we can make this work. Country music's power couple. Fuck, maybe even a real weddin' and everything." His eyes rake me up and down. "You're lookin' a hell of a lot sexier than the last time I saw you, so why the hell not?"

Oh. My. God.

I yank my hand out from under his. "Never. No way in hell."

He raises an eyebrow. "Never say never."

I turn to Morty and Jim. "My contract doesn't say anything about agreeing to something like that. Getting engaged is serious business, and you can't make me." I might sound like a petulant child, but I'm dead serious.

Jim, who puts off a fatherly air as opposed to Morty's slimeball vibe, smiles at me.

"Sit down, Holly. I think we can all come to an agreement here. You want what's best for your career, don't you?"

I take a deep breath, shoving down the urge to scream again.

"Yes. That's all I want. What's best for my career, and this can't be it."

"We've been in this business a lot longer than you have, darlin'. You need to trust us. We're not going to steer you wrong."

Patronizing. There it is again.

Morty starts carrying on like this is a done deal. "It's fucking perfect. JC, during your last song of the night, you'll call Holly up onstage and drop to one knee. People will eat that shit up."

"You can't do this!"

All three men look at me, and their smiles send chills down my spine.

Holy. Shit.

"Deal with it, Wix," Morty says with a smug smile. "This is happening, or you're on the first bus back to the trailer park. Maybe we'll even let you keep the diamond when it's all over."

Nothing I can say is going to change a thing right now, so instead, I swallow back the protests I want to scream and speak as calmly as I'm able. "This discussion isn't over, but I have to get to practice."

My head reeling and stomach churning, I pull my trucker hat lower and head for the door without waiting for a response.

"Let's take that one from the top again," I call out to my guys in the band.

I want to apologize for wasting their time today, but I don't because then I'd have to explain why—and I can't. But it's impossible to concentrate on the music when I feel my dream slipping away. *What won't I do to save it? Can I go through with this farce?* Everyone has a line, and I'm not sure where mine is.

But that's not a question I'm going to be able to answer right now, so I'd better freaking focus. We have a new song that we want to add to the set list, and if we can't get it together, we're all going to look like idiots at the next show.

I study the guys, and am once again thankful that Homegrown didn't screw me over on this front. My band is an amazing crew, and I'm lucky to have them. I could have ended up with a bunch of washed-up has-beens, but I got seasoned musicians with serious talent. Shocking, right?

The bitterness I feel toward Homegrown is ridiculous. It's so hard to reconcile the fact that I have them to thank for giving me a shot to live this dream, and now they're demanding I fall in line or sacrifice it. How is that fair? I guess it's lucky that I wasn't raised to think life should be fair. And besides, I've had my share of good fortune—if I didn't win *Country Dreams*, I'd still be serving up deep-fried pickles at the bowling alley.

And Gran might still be alive, the voice of guilt whispers in my brain.

"Holly, what the hell? You planning on singing anytime soon, darlin'?"

I jerk my head around, shaking the thought from my mind as the guys silence their instruments . . . several bars after my cue.

"Sorry. I was a million miles away."

"You need to take a breather, hon?" Lonnie, my drummer, asks as he spins one stick.

"Nah, I'm good. I just need to get my head back in the game."

The guys look at each other, and suddenly I wonder if there's something I'm missing.

"What?"

Darius, my bass player, finally speaks. "You getting homesick thinking about being away on Christmas Eve? Because we've all decided we're catching flights home on our own dime right after the show. You should do the same."

He's talking about our show in three days, the one that will finally get me onstage at Madison Square Garden in New York City. Talk about a completely different universe. Little old me from Gold Haven, Kentucky, opening for country's bad boy on a stage only slightly less impressive to me than the Opry itself. I just hope I don't develop stage fright.

I consider Darius's question. I'm a little homesick, but not because I want to go home—because I don't really have a home to go to anymore. The only family I had that mattered is six feet under. My first Christmas without Gran is going to be brutal. My first everything without her has been tough, so why should this be any less painful?

Maybe I deserve the pain. Maybe I earned that pain.

But wasting this opportunity isn't going to bring her back or absolve me of the guilt I'm carrying. Nothing will.

"You ready, Holly?"

I shake it all off as best I can—JC, the record execs, my guilt—and straighten my spine, standing taller in my worn-out boots.

"I'm ready. Let's take it from the top."

The rest of practice goes well because I force myself to stay firmly in this moment, firmly in the music. Singing my songs, even on this practice stage, is enough to finally drag me out of the dark place I've been sliding into.

As we pack up the gear when practice is finished, I check my watch. I'm headed back to Mick and Tana's for dinner, and then home to pack for the two shows we've got before our extended break. First stop Philly, and then the Big Apple.

I shrug my bag over my shoulder and feel it vibrate with a text. Fishing my phone out, I see one from Tana.

TANA: I thought you said you weren't doing it!!

I quickly tap out a reply.

ME: ??? are you talking about?

Tana's response doesn't hit my phone until I'm climbing into my car and firing it up.

TANA: JC. The engagement.

I called Tana as soon as I walked out of Homegrown and drove to practice. The number of f-bombs she dropped during that conversation was impressive. She almost beat out Mrs. Finchly, Gran's next-door neighbor, when the repo man came to take her shiny new convertible because her winnings at bingo weren't covering the payments.

Before I can type out a reply, my phone rings. Tana.

"I'm not," I answer.

"Um, honey, have you seen Perez Hilton? Because there's a picture of JC at the very top, and he's buying a fucking engagement ring. He's nothin' but smiles."

What? No way. No. Way.

"That's impossible. They just—"

"Hang up the phone and google it, Holly. It's there. It's happening. They're going to corner you into it, and they're not wasting any time. You need a plan."

"A plan?"

My brain spins, attempting to latch on to any idea at all, but I've got nothing. Nothing but the vision of me standing onstage at *Dick Clark's New Year's Rockin' Eve* celebration, the words "go screw yourself" popping out of my mouth when JC pops the question.

My career will be over. My dream will be dead.

Tana is right; I need a plan. Because boarding a bus home isn't going to be part of my future. I might be a lot of things, but a failure isn't one of them.

CHAPTER THREE

CREIGHTON

Christmas Eve, New York City

Bored.

It's not a safe state of affairs for a man like me. Bad shit happens when I'm bored. I have a tendency to dabble in hostile takeovers when I need something to get my adrenaline pumping. Or I'll go out and pick up three women, and introduce them to each other in the filthiest way possible.

Judge me all you want; I don't give a fuck what you think about me. Because I own half this town, and the other half isn't worth having.

You can check the crotch of my Gucci suit pants for yourself. Not even a hint of a bulge at the thought of a foursome. Threesomes are passé, but it's a sad situation when even a foursome can't get my dick interested.

Because I'm fucking bored.

I shove out of my chair and stalk to the window of my tower. You see that down there? Fifth Avenue and my city. We're just south of the park, which means the holiday lights are everywhere.

I fucking hate Christmas. Just one more holiday that reminds me of things I'd rather forget. But enough of this shit. Pulling my phone from my pocket, I hover my thumb over the screen. I've got hundreds of numbers I can call and have a chick on my dick in less than fifteen minutes, even on Christmas Eve. Again, I wait for some sign of action in my pants, but I get nothing.

My dick must be broken. There's no other explanation for it—except that I'm bored with my options. I know I'm getting repetitive, but bad things happen when I get bored. My past is littered with mistakes that arose from situations like this one.

But you know what? I'm in the mood to make another mistake. It's time to grab my suit jacket and find out what kind of trouble I can get into tonight.

CHAPTER FOUR

HOLLY

Christmas Eve, New York City

I'm giving myself a man for Christmas. Yes, a man.

I can do this. Really, I can. I think. Maybe.

From just inside the door, I scan the fancy hotel bar, looking for a likely prospect. The warmth of the whiskey I drank at the after party buzzes through me in a happy hum. I needed more than a little liquid courage to talk myself into this plan. I think it's safe to say that this *is* my first rodeo.

And of course, I had to choose something way out of my league. But who knew the hotel bar would be so dang fancy? The Rose Club at the Plaza. Fifth Avenue, New York City.

I stifle the urge to check the carpet for any traces of mud that might have fallen off my cowboy boots, and wonder if it's the first time a Kentucky girl in honest-to-

God shit-kickers has stepped into this joint. Although, these boots are part of my stage costume, so the fringe and rhinestone-encrusted leather is a heck of a lot nicer than the worn-out ones I left in my cubby on the bus.

The bluish-purple glow coming from the ornate domed light fixtures makes it look like someone dunked the whole room in grape juice, giving the bar a kind of otherworldly feel. One look at the handful of folks in here tonight makes it clear that these people are from a completely different planet than me.

But I push aside the comparison and venture closer to the shiny wooden bar. If I'm going to do this, I'm going to need another shot of that liquid courage.

I slide onto one of the velvet bar stools, absolutely aware of the fact that my tiny jean skirt is riding up my thighs. A man in a suit one stool down is eyeing my legs while he swirls the liquor in his glass. I can't tell what color it is, because everything takes on the unnatural shade of the lights.

I'm grateful for those lights. Something about the color is mellow and sexy, and it gives me the guts to follow through with my plan.

My Christmas list may be short, but it's certainly specific. One man with enough cockiness and a smok-ing-hot body to take my mind off the grief stalking me tonight.

I snag the drink menu and flip it open. It lands on exactly the page I need. *American Whiskey*. The best damn kind there is. My jaw drops when I read the prices.

"Holy shit. Sixteen dollars for Jack Daniel's? What the hell? Did Jack rise from the grave and make that mash himself? Holy . . . *damn*." My voice carries, and everyone in the room, including the bartender in his snazzy suit, turns to look at me.

The guy one seat over must take that as some sort of invitation, and slides onto the velvet stool next to me. His smile is as smarmy as his words.

"I'll buy a pretty girl a drink." He jerks his head toward the bartender. "Put whatever she wants on my tab."

Well, that didn't take long.

I drop my gaze quickly, and the paunch straining the buttons of his dress shirt quickly disqualifies him as having the smoking-hot body on my Christmas wish list. But maybe this is a situation where beggars can't be choosers?

I've never been much of a barfly, but the few times I've ventured out after shows with the guys, it seems like I always get these business types who spend a little too much time on the road, and none of it hitting the hotel gym.

Resignation filters through me. Maybe this is as good as it gets? One thing is clear, even through the warmth of the whiskey—this is the dumbest idea I've ever had.

"Thank you, but I think I'm a little lost tonight." I flip the menu shut. "I should probably just get back to my room."

The label put me up at the Plaza as a goodwill gesture for doing the show on Christmas Eve; otherwise, I would never drop that kind of money on a hotel, even if I had that kind of cash to spare—which I don't.

He lays a hand on my arm. "How can you be lost, when I just found you?"

The line is cheesy, and I'm not even sure it counts as a line. But either way, I'll be better off with some room-service dessert and a pity party for one.

I slide off the edge of the stool, but his grip tightens before his hand lands on my leg, sliding up my skirt almost instantly.

"You can't go yet. We haven't even gotten acquainted. Just let me buy you a drink. I promise I'll make it worth your while, sweetheart."

Chills of *ick* run through me at his touch, and I struggle to slide out of his grip, but he's got me trapped. Apparently he thinks I'm a hooker, but my skirt isn't *that* short.

Reaching down to pry his hand off my leg, I dig my nails in, but he just squeezes tighter.

Seriously, world? This is what I get when I try to have some harmless fun? Not. Fair.

I yank at his hand and open my mouth to tell him to let go when a rough, deep voice curls around me.

"I'll thank you to take your hands off my wife."

In one swift move, the unwelcome hands touching me are gone, and the man is stumbling off his stool. My gaze jerks from the handsy guy trying to catch his balance, and darts over my left shoulder.

Another guy in a suit. Except instead of being on the slippery side of fifty and overweight, this man might just be God's gift to women. Or maybe just Saint Nick's gift to me in the form of a rescue? Because, holy wow. Dark brown hair falls perfectly over his forehead, and his cheekbones could have been carved by one of those Italian master sculptor guys.

A hint of recognition tugs at the edges of my whiskey-soaked brain as his dark eyes burn into mine, as if daring me to play along. I don't know what his game is, but for him . . . I might just be willing to try it.

The sexy man in the suit lifts a hand to my hair and smooths a lock between two fingers. His dark brown eyes never leave mine. "Darling, I told you that the picking-up-strangers game to make me jealous was for New Year's Eve, not Christmas Eve."

The other guy backs away another step, and the memory of his touch is fading just as quickly as it came. It's like watching the laws of nature play: the beta male bows to the alpha, and the sexy man in the suit is one hundred percent the alpha dog in this situation.

Whatever pheromones he's throwing off have me shifting on the velvet bar stool and leaning closer to him without thinking. It's a million times better than the thought of getting up close and personal with Handsy. I reach down to rub my arm where the jerk touched me, and a red mark has already appeared.

Alpha Dog doesn't miss my move. He lays a possessive hand on my shoulder and speaks to Handsy in a low, dangerous growl. "If you don't want to be still picking up teeth next Christmas Eve, I'd suggest you pay your tab and get the fuck out of here before I lose my temper. You don't ever put your hands on a woman who clearly isn't interested."

Handsy apparently doesn't recognize the alpha yet. "She came in here looking like she was trolling for a man.

She was fucking interested. Maybe you should keep a leash on your woman if you can't control her."

I open my mouth to tell him I was most definitely *not* interested, but Alpha speaks first.

"I suggest you walk away while you're still able."

Alpha's expression must be even more dangerous than his words, because Handsy snaps his fingers at the bartender, who slides an embossed leather folder down the bar. Apparently he's been listening to this whole exchange as well, because he's grinning smugly.

Alpha slides an arm around my middle and pulls me back against his solid chest. It's everything I can do to stop myself from purring and rubbing up against him like a tabby cat in heat.

What is coming over me? I've never reacted like this to any man before. I should want to shower off the other guy, but instead I just want to get closer to the leader of the pack behind me.

Handsy flips the folder open and fumbles for his wallet.

Alpha Dog clips out, "Make sure you leave a good tip."

The other man is counting out bills, and Alpha Dog's thumb begins to rub a path back and forth across my stomach, just below my breasts. With every stroke, I press more weight back against him as all the nerve endings in my body seem to come to life at once.

His chest rumbles with his words. "Two hundred should be sufficient. It's fucking Christmas. Don't be a cheap fuck, you prick."

I bite my lip to hold back the giggle welling up inside me.

Handsy shoves two hundreds inside and flips the leather folder shut before stumbling off his stool.

He takes three steps, and Alpha says, "I sure as hell hope you haven't forgotten to apologize to my *wife* for being a dick before you go."

Handsy pauses and stiffens. "Sorry, ma'am. I apologize sincerely."

My belly shakes with silent laughter, and Alpha squeezes me tighter.

"Something funny, sweetheart?"

I'm debating whether I should disentangle myself from his hold to face him when he takes the decision out of my hands and drops his arm. He pulls out the bar stool next to me, unbuttons his suit jacket, and sits.

I expect him to turn and start explaining what just happened, and why the hell he rescued me and then pretended to be my husband, but he just holds up two fingers.

"Bushmills 21 for the lady."

The bartender hops to it, nodding before he grabs a tall bottle from the top shelf.

"I'll have a double shot of Jack," I say, correcting him.

The bartender freezes and looks from me to Alpha Dog.

My sideways glance reveals him shaking his head. "She'll have the Bushmills. We're expanding her palate."

I look at him and open my mouth to object, but get distracted by his profile. The man is beautiful, from his dark hair and equally dark eyes to his black tie tucked into a matching three-button vest. My eyes drop lower to the bulge in his suit pants. I swallow and remember exactly why I'm sitting in this bar tonight.

It hits me like a splash of slush from a cab on my boots. I know exactly who he is, because he doesn't look all that different from the cover of *Forbes* that Tana had at her house a couple of months ago. I still remember the headline: KARAS CRUSHES COMPETITION.

Well, he certainly crushed the competition tonight. The rush of nervousness I was already feeling builds. The *Holly gives herself a man for Christmas* plan is suddenly alive and well again.

But how do I do this? I've never propositioned a stranger in a bar, let alone a billionaire. Or is this already a foregone conclusion, and he's just waiting for me to catch up to his agenda for the evening?

"We're expanding my palate?" My words come out breathier than I intended.

His full lips slide into a lazy, yet predatory smile. "In this respect, and I'm hoping a few others before the night is over."

Oh. My. God.

I sure hope I know what I'm getting myself into.

CHAPTER
FIVE

CREIGHTON

uck me.

That's what her glossy siren-red lips are saying, and I don't think she has a goddamn clue how edible she looks sitting perched on that stool. She shifts, and the rhinestones at her neck, ears, and wrist flash purple in the trademark light of the Rose Club— light that's more accustomed to reflecting off diamonds than costume jewelry.

She drew my eye when she stepped through the door because she looked so utterly out of place. But I haven't been able to take my eyes off her because . . . Fuck. I have no idea. I've had my fair share of beautiful women, but this one's a completely different breed. Not the trained purebred type of woman who crowds this place, tittering and looking for her next meal ticket.

No. One look at her, and I know she's untrained and innocent. She's not the kind of woman who is going to be angling for a handout, and the absolute lack of motive behind her actions is more alluring than I would have guessed. The way she instantly played along and never shied from my touch. Hell, she leaned into me, wanting more. She's rare, and I'm the kind of man who appreciates that quality more than most when it comes to choosing a woman.

And then there's the fact that she's sitting in this bar on Christmas Eve with no ring on her finger—not sure how the dumb fuck missed the lack of that little accessory. It tells me she's as alone in this city tonight as I am.

Boredom is now the last thing on my mind. This innocent girl has managed to eradicate every trace of it.

I make my decision instantly. *She's mine tonight.*

The bartender, Aric, according to his nametag, sets our whiskey down in front of us.

"Please let me know if I can get you anything else, Mr. Karas."

I wince as he says my name. I expect her demeanor to change immediately, for greedy claws to come out and spear into me.

Instead, she eyes the lowball glass in front of her. "How much is that drink gonna cost me? Ten dollars a swallow?"

I barely hold back a groan at the word *swallow*, because, fuck, I'm a guy, and I've already been picturing my dick in her mouth.

"Not a thing, sweetheart. I wouldn't let a woman drink alone, and I sure as hell wouldn't let her pay for her own drinks."

I wait for an objection, but instead she lifts the glass and sniffs its contents.

"Kinda smells like . . . candy?"

"Caramelized toffee and dark chocolate."

Her lips press against the rim, and she tips back a swig. *Fuck.* Her throat works as she swallows the liquor.

I want to taste it on her lips. Hell, I just want to taste her. I lean in, not even totally conscious of my movement, but urged on by the need to sample my favorite Irish whiskey from her, rather than from the glass.

But she freezes, and so do I.

Her brown eyes widen. "Holy horseshit, that's some good stuff."

My chest shakes as a chuckle breaks loose. "Damn straight."

Her mouth curves into a grin as she lifts and sips again. This time she swallows more, and my dick pulses against the zipper of my suit pants. I want her on her knees, those wide brown eyes staring up at me as I cup her jaw and thrust my cock between those lush red lips.

"Take more," I say.

Her eyebrows lift, but she complies. Or she complies with what she thinks I want.

No, sweetheart. I'm just practicing what I'm going to say when I'm fucking your gorgeous face. She's too innocent to understand just yet, but she will.

My dick jumps again, and I know if I don't calm it down, I'll be stammering one-syllable words due to lack of oxygen in my brain. I've never reacted this quickly and this strongly to a woman before. It's gut-level and completely fucking primal, but I don't question it. I embrace it.

My mind is flipping through all the lines I can use to get her out of this bar and back to my penthouse for a long night of no-holds-barred, wake-the-neighbors fucking, when she beats me to it.

"Are you married? Other than to me on a purely fake basis?" she asks, a small smile curving her fuckable lips.

I don't have an explanation for playing the jealous-husband card except that she brought out my most basic possessive instincts. If they were any stronger, I would have been thrown out of the bar for pissing a circle around her to mark my territory, and challenging any man who thought he had big enough balls to take her from me.

That was a completely new and novel feeling. Normally my brain comprehends in this fashion: *Hot. Want to fuck.*

It's as simple as that. And nothing further.

Men are not complicated creatures, ladies. You're hot? Chances are, the guys you know want to fuck you. It's called human nature.

But it wasn't so simple with this fringed-cowboy-boot-wearing oddity. She's been a tantalizing breath of fresh air sweeping by me, and the urge to stake my claim burst forth from the primordial part of my brain.

Her smile fades, and I pull myself back to the conversation I'm supposed to be having with her. I forgot her question already.

"Why the frown, sweetheart?"

She stiffens on her stool. "One, don't call me sweetheart. And two, if you're married, you can take your fancy-whiskey-sippin' ass to another table."

I smirk. So that was the question. "Not married. Why, you looking for a husband?"

Her button nose wrinkles in distaste. "No. Absolutely not."

I lift one eyebrow. The women I know would consider that a proposal—even though it wasn't. And they would jump on it.

"You have a problem with the whole institution, or just with respect to yourself specifically?"

She takes another drink, a big one this time. She finishes draining her glass and sets it on the bar. Those brown eyes cut to mine.

"I didn't come here to talk about marriage. I came here to find a hot guy who looked like he could handle himself, and see where the night takes us." She lifts her glass again as if she needs another sip to fortify her next words, but it's already empty. She sets it on the table, and with a rush, says, "You think you might be that guy?"

I have the distinct impression that without the whiskey, she would never have been forward enough to speak those words. But this works perfectly with my plan. She's given me the opening I need, and I'm not the kind of man to screw up a perfect opportunity.

I lift my glass to my lips and swallow the contents before I slide it back onto the Rose Club cocktail napkin on the bar. I never break eye contact through the whole series of motions.

"Where are you from?" I don't usually ask questions, but with her, I want to know everything.

"Does it really matter?" she asks, and I can't tell if she's playing coy or if that's her natural state of being.

"I'm just wondering where they raise women who say

exactly what a man wants to hear when he's sitting next to a beautiful woman in a bar."

Her cheeks color with a pink blush, and I suspect it's not the whiskey. Her innocence rolls off her in waves. I want to see how far I can make that blush spread. I want to see the outline of my handprint on her ass in that same color.

I stand and hold out a hand. Her gaze drops to it, and she hesitates before laying her hand in mine.

Good girl.

I close my fingers around hers as she slides off the stool. Even with the heels of the boots, the top of her head barely clears my chin.

"Where are we going?" she asks.

"My place."

Her eyes widen. "I . . . I have a room. Here. I mean, if you want. Or, or—" She stammers over the words, and I know I need to put her at ease before she bolts.

I lift a hand to her chin and stroke her cheek with my thumb, tracing the sexy-as-hell flush. "Yes. I absolutely want."

She swallows and nods.

She's mine.

I don't want to release her, but I do. After pulling the money clip from the inside front pocket of my suit jacket, I peel off a few hundreds. I can't tip less than that bastard, or I'll be a total schmuck. I push them under the edge of my empty glass and pause, pull out another few bills, and motion for the bartender.

"Yes, sir?"

"We'll take a new bottle of Bushmills." I glance down

I meet his eyes. "No. No second thoughts."

"Good."

The single word sends shivers of excitement flickering through me. This man calls to me on a very basic level. It makes no sense. I mean, since when did suit-wearing billionaires turn me on? Usually, outside of the odd drunk fan, it's the dorky guys who hit on me, and there are *no* sparks.

How can I be turned on knowing how absolutely and completely out of my league he is?

My stomach flops like a whole mess of spring peeper frogs have been unleashed. I wasn't even this nervous when I stepped onstage for the first time on *Country Dreams*. Maybe this is what a minor league rookie feels like the first time he sets foot on the field of the big leagues.

I glance down at where he has a grip on my hand, and can't help but notice the bulge in the front of his suit pants.

Oh Lordy. What am I getting myself into? He's probably had his fair share of supermodels, and heck, any woman he's ever wanted. And now he's got *me*. Old insecurities sneak out of the shadows. I'm not good enough for this man, and I know it.

We step into the elevator, and my heart is hammering against my chest so loudly that I wonder if he can hear it. I forget that I'm still staring at his package when his hand once again lifts my chin.

"See something you like?"

My cheeks heat with a furious blush, and I raise my gaze to his amused one.

Oh my God. He caught me ogling his package. Fail, Holly! Fail.

"Uh . . ."

"Don't worry. I don't mind."

With his words, his thumb strokes along my cheekbone. It's such a familiar touch, and brings back the urge to just lean into him and let him take over.

Who am I kidding? Like I was ever in control of this encounter.

"What's your name, sweetheart?"

I grit my teeth at the throwaway endearment. I hate being called "hon" or "sweetheart"—my gran's favorite endearments—by someone I don't know. It seems so fake, and once again reminds me of what I've lost.

"No names," I say quickly.

His dark eyebrows shoot up nearly to his hairline. "Really? You don't want to know mine?"

It's not really fair of me, because I already know his, but I answer anyway. "None. I don't need to know your name."

He studies me for a few beats before replying with only a brief nod.

As soon as the doors open on my floor, he grabs me by the hand and pulls me out of the elevator, and I think I've reached the point of the evening where shit is getting real.

Equal amounts of apprehension and anticipation rush through me when he growls, "Which room?"

Oh God. What am I doing? Oh, wait, that's right. I'm about to have a one-night stand with a billionaire. *Get in the game, Holly. You can do this.*

"Um, 1919."

"Key?"

I slip my hand into the back pocket of my jean skirt and pull it out. Lifting it from my fingers, he pulls me down the hall in the direction of the room.

At least I don't need to worry about having to take the lead, because I have a feeling Creighton Karas is going to be just as demanding and dominant in the bedroom as he's rumored to be in the boardroom.

Gulp.

CHAPTER SEVEN

CREIGHTON

I need to take this slow. I need to take my time with her. She's the type of woman to be savored and appreciated, but I want to taste her innocence on my lips too badly to even try.

I have her ass filling my hands and her back up against the wall before the door clicks shut behind us and the bottle of whiskey thuds to the floor. I take her mouth, sliding my tongue between her bright red lips. *Fuck.* So damn sweet, just like I knew she would be.

Her quiet moan goes straight to my balls. I rock into her, my cock pressing against her pussy. She whimpers and bucks against me, her instincts coming on strong, despite her innocence. I reach down and wrap one leg around me, and she catches on quickly, repeating the movement with her other leg. Her skirt bunches up around her waist, and the heels of her boots dig into my ass. My need to fucking devour this woman jacks up higher as her nails dig into my shoulders to steady herself.

Don't worry, sweetheart. I'm not letting you go anywhere.

I bury one hand in her hair, tilting her head back to meet my gaze. "When I let you down from here, you're going to strip off everything but your boots and your panties, and get on your hands and knees on the bed."

Her dark eyes widen, clearly telegraphing her shock at my words.

Oh, this is going to be fun.

I begin to lower her to the ground, but her legs tighten around my waist.

I tighten my grip in her hair. "Do you understand me?"

She nods.

"Words. Yes or no?"

"Yes," she whispers.

The smile that spreads across my face feels predatory, even to me. "You're going to be a naughty fucking girl for me, aren't you?"

Her mouth opens to respond, but instead of speaking, she closes it and swallows—like she'll soon be swallowing my cock. She's going to be perfect.

"Do you want to know what I do to naughty girls?"

She nods.

"Anything I want."

Her pupils dilate, and I know I've got her exactly where I want her. My lips lower to hers and devour her again. The taste of whiskey reminds me that I want to lick it off her body, and drink it from her sweet pussy.

Fuck. What is it about this woman that makes me lose every shred of self-control?

I don't care enough to answer the question because

she's wrapped her hand around my neck, pulling me closer. Her quick little tongue tangles with mine, and the taste of her . . . Jesus. It steals away logic and common sense.

I yank myself back from the edge, and away from her lips, and slowly lower her to the ground.

"What—?" Her half protest is weak, and she presses a palm against my chest for balance.

"Now," I say, and wait for her to react.

"What?" she asks again, this time with more fortitude.

"I told you where I wanted you. And I want it now."

She blinks, as if trying to throw off the haze of desire.

I don't think so. I drop my hands to her shoulders and turn her to face the bed.

"Strip. Leave the panties and the boots. I want your ass in the air."

I release her, and she stumbles forward a step. I lock down the urge to steady her, because if I touch her again, I'm going to be tearing every thread she's wearing off her.

To her credit, she steadies herself—and quickly. I wonder how rapidly she's going to comply with my orders, but I don't have to wonder long. She reaches for the hem of her shirt and hesitates, glancing back over her shoulder.

Keep going, I think, waiting to see how well she'll comply with my orders—spoken and unspoken.

She bites her lip and looks forward again before slowly lifting the shirt up and over her head. It dangles from her fingertips for a moment before she drops it to the floor. She pauses, and I wonder if she's going to back out. But she doesn't. The sound of the zipper comes, and she shimmies her skirt off. A tiny red thong reveals most of her perfect peach of an ass.

Jesus fucking Christ, she's perfect.

"The bra too," I remind her when she drops her arms to her sides.

She shoots another glance back at me before reaching her arms around to unhook it and slide it off. It joins the pile of clothes on the floor. Her thumbs hook into the waistband of her thong.

"Stop."

She freezes when I utter the word.

"You need to learn to listen better, naughty girl. Leave them. I want you on the bed on your hands and knees, your ass in the air."

Her gaze snaps to the bed, and she takes a shaky step toward it. I move forward in one lunge, tearing the spread off it and tossing it aside.

Her hands hit the sheets as she stumbles forward. She stills for only a moment before crawling onto the bed and complying with my command.

"I'm going to rip those flimsy little panties right off you and eat that juicy cunt for dessert."

When her entire body shivers at my words, I wonder if anyone has ever spoken so crudely to her. I highly doubt it.

But still, she doesn't move. Doesn't make a break for it, so I'm all in.

CHAPTER EIGHT

HOLLY

His words. Oh my God, his *words*. I've read things like that, but I've never heard someone say them. So dirty, so filthy . . . and God help me, so *hot*. Maybe there's something wrong with me, but I like it. I want him to tell me what to do, because if he can make me feel this way with nothing but words and a few kisses, I want more.

I watch out of the corner of my eye as he shrugs off his suit jacket and tosses it on a chair at the edge of the room. His cufflinks clink as they hit the top of the dresser. His hands don't slow as they unbutton the shirt and toss it on top of the suit jacket. He strides toward the bed, and heat flares within me.

I'm expecting a soft touch, a caress, but instead his hand cracks across my naked butt cheek. The sting shoots up my body, followed by a hot, sensual burn.

An undignified squeak escapes my lips as I lower my ass out of the strike zone. But I don't move fast enough.

Another smack catches the same cheek, but lower, where it meets my thigh.

"Why—" I start, but his big hand covers the sting, silencing me. A possessive squeeze of his palm is followed by his thumb sliding up and under the waistband of my panties.

"I'm keeping these," he says before snapping the delicate lace of my panties and letting them flutter down my left leg. Another tug and they're gone. "And I'm punishing you for hesitating to follow my orders. And because I've been dying to see my handprint on your ass since you first blushed in the bar."

Once again, his words send a rush of desire through me unlike anything I've ever felt before—until his palm slides between my legs and cups me before dragging a single thick finger through my wetness.

He groans. "You're fucking drenched for me. Jesus."

His fingertip swirls my opening, teasing me. My thighs flex, and when he dips just barely inside, my inner walls clench, greedy and wanting to be filled.

What is happening to me? I push myself against his hand, and for a moment, he fills me. His hand drops away, and a cool rush of air precedes a light slap to my pussy.

"Wha—"

"My greedy girl is getting ahead of herself. I'll give you what you need, but you'll take it my way."

When I exhale sharply, another firmer smack lands in the same spot. And then he grips my hips and flips me onto my back in a single movement.

My head is still spinning from the abrupt change in

position, but my eyes track him as he leaves the edge of the bed, moves toward the entryway to the room, crouches low, and then returns.

He kneels at the base of the bed, grips my knees, and pulls me so my ass is almost hanging off the edge and my boot-clad ankles are resting on his shoulders. I'm completely and utterly exposed to him, and uncertainty fills me for a breath.

He lifts something, and in the dim light of the room, I see it's the bottle of whiskey. Never dropping my gaze, he opens it and drops the cap.

Um . . . strange time for a drink?

He leans in close, and his breath teases my center. "I wasn't done drinking earlier. So now I'm going to drink from this sweet little cunt and get drunk on you."

Again his filthy words send shivers through me, and his meaning dawns in my lust-handicapped brain. *He's going to what?*

I don't have time to question, because within moments he tips the bottle. Chilly liquid hits me and trickles down . . . into his mouth. He catches the whiskey on his tongue, lapping up my wetness at the same time.

Oh my God. Oh my God.

Pleasure spikes through me as he sucks and nips and licks until I can't help but lift my hips and buck against his mouth, wanting more and more of this sensation.

He stills, the liquid stops, and he lifts his mouth away.

"Wh—"

"You're not going to come until I give you permission. I'm going to enjoy my dessert first."

My nipples pucker, and arousal raises goose bumps along every inch of my skin.

"Okay," I whisper. "Please don't stop. Please."

I don't know who this senseless creature is who's begging a man to keep pouring whiskey on her lady bits, but I honestly don't care. I expect him to resume his actions, but he does something else, something completely unexpected.

He lowers the rim of the bottle to drag along my clit. The cool glass sends spikes of pleasure ripping through me.

He's not going to . . . he wouldn't . . . My imagination flies into a frenzy when he continues to drag the mouth of the bottle lower. And lower. It presses against my opening, but goes no further. He pulls the bottle away and presses it to his lips and drinks.

His Adam's apple bobs as he sucks down the liquor, and my throat dries to dust. It seems he can read my every thought, because he lowers the whiskey and leans forward, pressing my legs toward my body.

The bottle hovers over my mouth.

"Open."

He tilts it toward my lips, and I comply with his instructions in time for the whiskey to hit my tongue. I swallow until he stops the flow, and just when I've relaxed a fraction, he lowers again into his crouched position and a thick, blunt finger slides inside me without warning.

The liquor burns a path down to my belly, and red-hot need flares up from where he fills me. His dark eyes are locked on mine as he continues to thrust in and out with his finger and lowers his mouth to my clit.

And he feasts.

I'm riding high on the wave toward orgasm when a second finger pushes inside me for a moment before sliding lower.

Whoa. I flinch against the foreign feeling as his fingertip circles the pucker of my ass. I open my mouth to protest, but the sensation falls away and is replaced by his teeth nipping at my clit.

A moan rips from my throat as an orgasm rips through my body.

When I blink my eyes open, he's standing over me. He must have lowered my legs from his shoulders, even though I didn't realize it. His belt is undone, his pants are unzipped, and his hand is wrapped around a giant cock. I haven't seen that many in real life, but even I can recognize a monster when I see it.

"You want my cock?"

The bold question takes me off guard. "Um . . ."

"I asked you a question."

He's stroking himself from root to tip, waiting for my answer.

I nod.

But that's not enough for him.

"Tell me you want me to fuck that tight little cunt until you're still feeling it tomorrow."

"I—I want you to fuck me."

The words feel so foreign on my tongue, even though it's exactly what I wanted when I set foot in the bar. To find a man with enough confidence to give me exactly what I want. I just didn't expect to find *him*.

"Not good enough. You were looking for a man tonight, that much was clear. So ask for what you really want." He lowers his face to mine. "Because I'll give you all that and more."

I suck in a breath. He's right. Tonight is about me taking something I want and banishing the guilt chasing me. I grab my courage and push up on my elbows, bend my knees, and let my legs fall open.

"I want to still be feeling you tomorrow."

A devastating smile spreads across his face. "Good. Because you will."

He kicks off his shoes and shoves his pants to the floor. I expect him to pounce on me, but he snatches up his pants and fishes his wallet out.

Shoot. I totally forgot to grab the condoms out of my drugstore bag in the bathroom. Apparently I'm not good at this whole one-night stand thing.

But since I probably won't be doing it again anytime soon, I'm not going to worry about that. It's just one more reason to get everything from this night I possibly can before letting it fade into a distant memory.

CHAPTER NINE

CREIGHTON

She's sweetly submissive and everything I crave. Her inner battle between hesitation and need rages so strongly, I can see it in her eyes. It ratchets up my need to possess her . . . more than I remember ever wanting to possess something in a long, long time.

But that's all the time for introspection we have, folks, because I've got a condom on my dick and the sweetest pussy I've ever tasted in front of me begging me to pound into it.

My brain short-circuits when she slides one hand down toward her clit and strums it with her thumb. Now that, I didn't see coming.

Oh no, you don't, baby girl. That pussy became mine the second we entered the room. She needs to understand whose rules she's playing under.

"You touch yourself again and I'm going to spank that cunt until you come, and then I'm going to fuck you until you can't walk."

Her hand stills, and her eyes widen in shock. The innocent surprise in her eyes is quite possibly the most erotic thing I've ever seen. But as much as I'm loving those eyes, I want her back in the position I initially envisioned fucking her in.

"Get back on your hands and knees."

She blinks a few times, but follows my order.

Goddamn, that ass is a work of art. I smooth my hands over it, cupping each cheek. I slide my dick between her legs, coating myself in her slick heat.

Does she realize she's pushing her ass toward me? I can't help but smack it again.

Her whimpers and moans shear through my remaining threads of self-control. I wanted to take it slow, tease her to the brink, but I can't wait. I fit my cock to her opening and bury myself to the hilt in one thrust.

"Oh my God," she whispers, and I can hardly hear it over the blood pounding in my ears.

I can't move. Can't breathe. I'm gripped by the tightest, hottest pussy my cock has ever had the pleasure to know. It's a fucking religious experience. And yes, I'm aware I'm going to hell. It takes me several moments to gather myself and hold back the orgasm rising in my balls already.

Fuck. This woman could unman me, but that's not fucking happening.

I pull back and pump into her, fucking her with long, sure strokes. Her inner muscles flutter and clutch at my cock as I angle to hit her G-spot. She's clawing at the sheets and meeting my every stroke by pushing her ass back against me in perfect rhythm.

She rides the same wavelength as me, even as she rides my dick. It's carnal fucking poetry, and I've never felt anything like it in my life.

I decide to push her further. I slide one hand around her hips and tease her clit with my thumb. She clenches tighter, harder, and I fight to keep my orgasm in check. I swirl my thumb lower, coating it in her slickness. Her tight little asshole is teasing me as I fuck her, and I can't stem the urge to get a little piece of that too. I pull my hand away.

"Touch yourself. I want your fingers on that little clit of yours, but don't fucking come until I tell you to."

Her head jerks in what I assume is a response, and I grip both hips with my hands before sliding my slick thumb to her ass. The moment I circle the pucker, she stills.

I wait for the protest . . . but it never comes.

I continue thrusting and she resumes her counterthrust, and maybe even tilts her ass higher, further baring my target. I would bet my company that she's never been touched there. When my thumb breaches the tight ring of muscle, her moans turn to plaintive screams, and her cunt clamps down on my dick in a stranglehold.

"Fuck!" One more thrust. Two. And I'm lost.

I shoot my load, and for the first time in my entire adult fucking life, I feel like it drains every single brain cell from my body.

We both collapse onto the bed, and I roll us sideways so I'm not crushing her with my weight.

She doesn't even realize it, but this nameless woman

just brought me to my knees. And I can't fucking wait to experience it all over again.

I wake slowly, rolling over to reach for the woman beside me as I had three other times last night, but my hand hits cold, empty sheets. My eyes snap open to confirm what I'm feeling.

She's gone.

I sit up in bed, shove a hand through my hair, and survey the room. No sign that she's ever been here.

Rolling out of bed, I pull on my crumpled suit pants, wrap a hand around my morning wood, and squeeze it in an effort to calm it down. I'd prefer to be going for round number five with *her*, but she's fucking gone.

I pull on my shirt, telling myself that I don't care, and if she were any other ordinary one-night stand, I wouldn't. But last night was anything but ordinary.

And I wasn't fucking done with her yet.

My inner monologue sounds altogether too close to a petulant child, but when you get to my level of wealth and success in life, you get used to having pretty much whatever the hell you want.

And I want her—right now, tomorrow, and until I've had enough—which I can't imagine happening anytime soon.

I check the bathroom. Nothing. Not even a stray hairpin or smear of makeup on the counter.

Grabbing my wrinkled suit jacket, I let myself out of

the room. There's nothing but a destroyed bed and used condoms left inside anyway.

At the front desk, no amount of bribes or threats will get the name the reservation was made under. Apparently the Plaza prides itself on always offering the utmost privacy for all its guests.

Moralistic bastards.

Frustration grips me until my Machiavellian brain begins to formulate a plan. I refuse to admit defeat.

My lips tug with a smile. I know exactly how I'm going to handle this.

Merry fucking Christmas to me.

I just hope my "wife" is ready for what's about to happen.

CHAPTER
TEN

HOLLY

"**A**nd tonight's top story: Billionaire playboy Creighton Karas has published a missed connection that has gone viral, and there's no doubt as to why. Most of it we can't read on the air, but the gist of it is, he spent Christmas Eve with a woman who he claims is going to be the next Mrs. Creighton Karas. The posting requests that the lady in question, whose name and number he didn't get prior to or following their . . . encounter, show up at midnight on December 31st at the location of the tryst, which he claims only this particular lucky lady would know. Mr. Karas will be waiting with an engagement ring—and prenup—in hand."

The green power smoothie in my hands falls to the floor of my tiny kitchen, the glass shattering on the tile and coating it with swampy goo as I gape at the TV.

Oh. My. God.

He didn't.

He did.

Holy. Shit.

My cell phone rings, and I blindly grope the countertop for it. I don't bother looking at the display. I know exactly who it is.

"Please don't start screaming, Tana."

Instead of the screeches I expect to hear, my friend speaks very calmly. "Holly, they're talking about you on TV, but they don't know they're talking about you on TV."

"Yeah. I figured that one out myself."

"Please tell me you're going to go," she says.

"Are you serious?" I screech.

It was just supposed to be one night. A Christmas Eve fling. No one was supposed to know. Well, no one but me, the guy in question, and Tana, who demanded all the details when I told her I had a single amazing night with her potential backup husband.

"Holly—"

"What do you think would happen to my career if I did this?"

Tana is silent for a few beats before she answers. "It might be exactly what you need to get out of the disaster with JC. New Year's Eve in New York, baby. You can go one way or the other."

Holy crap, she's right. But still . . .

"The label? My contract? What about those minor details?"

Homegrown will blackball me and find some way to slap me with a breach-of-contract suit if I don't show up to this New Year's Eve farce with JC and let him propose.

"Creighton Karas has enough money to buy your way out of your contract, if not the entire damn label. And he wants to marry you!"

I'm not sure why Tana is a dreamy-eyed romantic all of a sudden, but it's misplaced. Either way, I'm now a cynical realist when it comes to things like my career.

Besides, Creighton Karas does *not* want to marry me because he's in love with me. He's probably in lust after all the things I let him do *to* me four days ago. *All those things* . . . I wasn't even able to give Tana all the details because I was too dang embarrassed to put them into words.

My body heats just remembering. I'm still not sure where I found the courage.

Oh, that's right—whiskey.

"He doesn't want to marry *me*, he wants to marry my . . . pussy." Crass, but it's probably the truth. "With a prenup. And with his track record, that prenup is going to come into play sooner rather than later."

After spending that night with him—the one where I left him buck naked and asleep in bed while I hopped in a cab to JFK, I did just the tiniest bit of research. All it took was one Google search to find out a heck of a lot.

Honestly, though, after reading the first few entries, I had to make myself stop. It didn't matter because I was never going to see him again—not outside the zillions of pictures of him with other women. I also wasn't the biggest fan of reading about his *love 'em and leave 'em* ways. Including his ex-wife, Shaw MacLeod, CEO of the chain of luxury MacLeod resorts.

"What the fuck ever," Tana says. "Does it really make a difference? It's *Creighton Karas*."

"And I'm Holly Wix. I can't take a chance this will

blow up in my face, and I'll never get to sing anywhere but the bowling alley on karaoke night again."

Even though Monty said he'd screw my life over so badly I'd never even sing there again. Not singing isn't an option. This is my life. My passion. Everything I have left in this world that truly matters. And because of that, I have to be smart.

"Lay it all out there when you go meet him," Tana says. "See what he says. He's already gone this far, so I doubt he'll argue too much. He's the one who'll look like an idiot if this stunt of his doesn't work. I think you've got leverage; you might as well use it."

I think about her point. Leverage. That's something I've never really had before. But still, the idea of marrying a guy I've met once? It's insane. Certifiable. Almost as insane as the label thinking I should get engaged to JC.

Why do both of my options involve a diamond ring?

I squeeze my eyes shut, wanting to run back to a tour bus, climb on, and pretend none of this ever happened. I just want to *sing*, damn it.

"Holly? You still there?"

"Sorry, I'm . . . thinking."

"What's there to think about? Marry a billionaire with a giant cock, or get engaged to a has-been who will almost certainly ask you to try fucking him in the ass with a strap-on."

"Tana! Jeez. Don't ever say that." But her blunt words give me more to think about. "I don't even know the guy."

"You don't know either of them, but that didn't stop

you from sleeping with the oh-so-sexy Creighton Karas," she unhelpfully points out.

I sigh. "You know why I did."

"I know. But still, what do you have to lose?"

Everything, I want to say. But I don't.

My first one-night stand, and the guy had to screw it up by telling the world through some PR stunt of a marriage proposal. I guess that's what happens when you pick a demanding billionaire.

"You know what I do with naughty girls? Whatever I want."

I still remember the conversation, and my nipples pucker in my bra. How can he still have this effect on my body? That can't be normal.

"Holly?"

"I'm thinking."

"You're taking that flight to New York either way, aren't you?" she asks.

I squeeze my eyes shut. I'm backed into a corner, and I don't see a way out other than these two very crazy options laid out in front of me.

I have no idea what I'm going to do. Still, I have to do something. I have no other choice.

With a deep breath, I reply, "Yes. I'm taking the flight to New York."

CHAPTER
ELEVEN

CREIGHTON

I would have made an excellent warlord.

I see.

I want.

I conquer.

I keep.

Anyone who gets in my way is removed by whatever means necessary. I'm not afraid to take chances, and I'm sure as hell not afraid to make waves.

The only time I let something go is when I'm damn good and ready, and there's no guarantee I'll ever be ready when it comes to the woman I'm waiting on. The last six days have done nothing but strengthen my determination to have her on my terms.

I've made myself comfortable in a leather wingback chair in Room 1919 of the Plaza, enjoying three fingers of Bushmills while I wait for my newest acquisition to arrive. Because in all honesty, at this point, that's exactly what she is. The latest toy to add to my collection.

Cannon Freeman, my best friend and COO, would

probably tell me that calling my bride-to-be an acquisition is the quickest way to fuck this up, and he'd be right. I may think it, but I'm not stupid—I'd never say it to her face.

Yes, I know I sound like an asshole. It goes with the territory. You don't get where I am in life without making more enemies than you can count. But one of the upsides? I get to pull crazy stunts like this, and people just shake their heads and wish they could be me.

There's no guarantee she shows, but I've wagered big many times before—and won big. Honestly, I don't expect this time to be any different.

She slipped out of this very room in the early hours of Christmas morning, leaving me without any way to track her down. I'm a creative guy, so I took a novel approach to finding her.

I sip the whiskey as I wait and listen to CNN. The topic of conversation on this New Year's Eve? You guessed it, yours truly. But I'm no stranger to being discussed by talking heads. Although, the conversation on the screen is starting to piss me off.

"This kind of behavior by a CEO does nothing to inspire the confidence of his stakeholders. Once again, I urge that the activist investors come together and take a stand."

Usually I ignore these kinds of opinions, but when it's your uncle on CNN bitching about the way you run your company and insulting your character, it's harder to let it slide. Especially when it's the uncle who begrudgingly took you and your sister into his home and "raised" you. I throw the mental quotes around the word raised because I'm not sure shoving me off to boarding school and turning my sister over to a nanny counts as raising us.

Either way, every public company deals with activist shareholders; they're just not usually relatives. I'll deal with him later. He's made noises for a while, and it seems it's time to shut him up for good.

I look at the clock on the bottom of the screen: 11:50. Ten minutes to go. She'll show. My missed connection wasn't a question, it was an order, and she's very good at doing what she's told. And once she comes, she'll continue to concede to my every wish, because that's how things work in my life. I give the commands, and everyone else obeys.

CNN cuts to a commercial, and then my uncle is back spewing more bullshit. I glance at the clock again: 11:58. The woman sure knows how to make a man wait. I wonder if she realizes she's going to be punished if she's late.

The thought brings a smile to my face.

CHAPTER TWELVE

HOLLY

"I don't know what to do, Tana. I wish you'd pick up. I'm freaking out here!"

I whisper-yell the words into my phone, knowing I'm being unfair because I know she has an appearance at the Opry tonight. But still, if there was any time I could use her guidance, it would be right now.

I sold my soul to the record company for what turned out to be chump change, but I got the chance to live my dream. What am I willing to do to save that dream? That's the question I've asked myself over and over for the last forty-eight hours.

I'm here in Manhattan, feeling like I've just watched the last grains of sand pass through the hourglass. I'm out of time.

A feeling of inevitability mixed with helplessness weighs down on me, and I hate it. When it comes to my career, I want to be in the driver's seat. I don't want someone else calling the shots. But that's not a choice I get to make.

I look down one last time at the list in my hand. Pros and cons. Because apparently that's what you do when faced with a decision like this. Weigh the options.

Get engaged to JC and perpetuate a farce that may end up with me being an even bigger laughingstock in the industry, but keep the record execs happy and my career flowing in the right direction.

My other choice is to sell my body to a man for a generous divorce settlement in the hopes that he has enough power to save me from the wrath that will surely follow from the record label.

I'll possibly be putting my dream at risk, but I have to believe Tana is right—the man is rich beyond my wildest imagination, and with that money comes incredible power. Will he use it to help me?

The other pro on that side of the column is the amazing sex. But will I be able to have that kind of relationship while keeping myself and my emotions intact? He was so incredibly dominant before, and I can't imagine he'll be anything less on a daily basis. But will he understand that the demands on my career come first?

Do I take the safe road? Or do I take the bold one?

"Sixty! Fifty-nine! Fifty-eight!"

My belly flops as the countdown to the New Year begins.

I suck in a deep breath and let it out. And I start to run.

CHAPTER
THIRTEEN

HOLLY

Heart hammering, I lift my hand to knock, but before my knuckles connect with the surface, the door swings open.

And there he is.

Tall and darkly handsome in a black suit, crisp white shirt, and thin black tie. Silver cufflinks pin his French cuffs in place, and a heavy silver watch peeks out from beneath, settling against his thick, tanned wrist. The minute hand on that watch should just be sliding past the mark of the midnight hour. I made it just in time.

I drag my gaze up the length of his tie until I reach his face. Even in my high-heeled boots, he's still several inches taller than me.

He's not looking at my face, though; he's making a leisurely study of the rest of me. Even though I just did the same thing, his gaze sends prickles of heat through me as I wait for him to finish. I count to fifteen before he finally meets my eyes.

His deep brown irises give nothing away, and neither

does his expressionless face. A five o'clock shadow darkens his jaw, which makes him even more danger-ously gorgeous than I remember.

"On time like a good girl. You just saved yourself a punishment."

The prickling heat spreads at the approval in his tone, although I think I hear a trace of disappointment at the lack of punishment. The memory of his palm connecting with my rear flashes through my brain, and I fight to keep my composure.

"Come in," he says before stepping back and holding the door open wide.

Following his command, I walk inside, attempting to hide the strange combination of anticipation and misgiving racing through me.

The door shuts with a decisive thud, and the metallic click of the dead bolt seems to echo in the silence of the room. Or maybe that's just my wildly overactive imagi-nation, which is replaying everything that happened in this room that night. It's like the reverse walk of shame, or returning to the scene of a crime.

Stop. Pull it together, Holly.

I walk to the window and stare down nineteen stories toward Central Park. Christmas lights and people are everywhere, celebrating the New Year. And out there in a studio on Times Square, there's a very unhappy JC and some livid record executives.

I had to shut my phone off hours before, turning it on only to call Tana, and powering it down immediately after. I told them I'd show up if I thought I could live with the decision, but it turns out, I can't.

And so now I'm here.

I feel him behind me, even though I didn't hear him cross the room. I tear my gaze away from the lights and turn to face him.

Taking a steadying breath, I say the only thing I can think of. "You sure know how to get a girl's attention."

His full lips quirk into a half smile before smoothing back into their expressionless line. Even the serious expression fuels the heat building in my core. I don't understand this man's effect on me. It makes no sense.

"I knew it would work." He holds out a hand. "I'll take your jacket."

His deep baritone rumbles through me, and my hands automatically reach for the buttons of my pea coat, even though I should be bristling at his certainty that I'd show. How could he know that? He doesn't know *me*.

He waits in silence for me to undo the buttons and hand it over. I focus on his eyes as they flick down to take in my skinny jeans tucked into fringed brown leather boots—my favorite pair and a rare indulgence, which I wore for a boost of confidence—and sheer white top and white cami beneath it. The rhinestones hanging from my ears and circling my wrist are costume jewelry, and this man is clearly used to spending time with women wearing diamonds. I'm obviously underdressed.

Why didn't I take something from my stage clothes to wear? A sexy dress, or a short skirt? Something that wouldn't remind me of my humble upbringing as he surveys me. You can take the girl out of the trailer park . . .

Pushing the thought away, I straighten my shoulders

and hand over my coat. He drapes it over the back of a chair with efficient movements and turns to face me once more. A briefcase sits on the desk, and I wonder if the notorious prenup is inside.

This is insane, I tell myself. But desperate times . . .

I try to lighten the mood by gesturing to myself. "I guess this isn't exactly what you were expecting."

"You wore a skirt last time."

I'm not sure what to make of that. "Yeah, well, I figured if you're serious at all about this, you should see something that approaches the real me, which is nothing fancy. The only time I generally go for anything special is when I'm onstage."

A flash of surprise spreads across his face, but he locks it away as quickly as it came. His next question surprises the hell out of me.

"Are you a stripper?"

I can't help but laugh. Given where I come from, that's not really a bad guess. A little devil on my shoulder takes control of my mouth.

"Is your offer contingent on me not being a stripper?" I automatically reach up to twirl my hair in what I assume is a stripper-like mannerism.

He considers the question for a moment. "I suppose not."

I smile, but I'm shocked by his reply. Really? Creighton Karas would marry a stripper?

"Why would you—"

My question is cut off when he says, "You didn't answer me."

I drop the lock of hair and lower my hands to my

sides. Not fidgeting under his direct stare takes all my effort.

"No, Mr. Karas, I'm not a stripper."

I could swear he breathes a sigh of relief at my answer, but his expression never changes.

"You have me at a disadvantage then. You clearly know my name, but I don't know yours."

Here we go. "My name is Holly Wickman, but most people know me as Holly Wix."

I'm not a big enough deal that I would expect recognition to light his features, but I'm slightly disappointed at the continued lack of change in his expression.

Finally, one arrogant eyebrow lifts as if telling me to continue. I stay quiet.

He fails to keep a slight edge of frustration out of his tone with his next question. "And why do most people know you as a name other than your own?"

"It's my stage name. I sing. Country music." The explanation comes out in a disjointed tumble of words.

Knowledge flares in his eyes. Has he heard of me? For some reason, that sends a shiver up my spine.

He frowns and his eyes turn hard. "I have heard of you. My assistant is a fan of yours, and your boyfriend who was . . . supposed to propose tonight?" He turns and reaches for my coat. "I make it a policy not to fuck other men's women. And I sure as fuck don't marry them. I would've married a stripper, but even I draw the line at a cheating whore."

The complete one-eighty in his mood throws me for a loop, and I cringe. "Please don't call me that."

"If the cowboy boot fits . . ." His expression is no longer blank, but filled with ugliness.

My stomach drops to my toes, and I take my coat from his outstretched hand.

Well, that was quick. And now I'm screwed.

"I knew it was a mistake to come here," I whisper.

"Then why did you?" he asks. "And why the hell did you leave that bar with me on Christmas Eve if you had a fucking boyfriend?"

I walk to the door, static buzzing in my head. I just bet it all on him, and *lost*.

What am I going to do now?

I grasp the handle, twist, and tug before I realize the door is still locked. I flip the dead bolt and pull it open an inch before a large tanned hand slaps against the door, slamming it shut.

"Answer me," he demands.

I don't care if he is a billionaire, I won't let anyone speak to me that way. Spinning around, I find myself trapped in the cage his arms have formed around me.

"You really want to know why I did what I did on Christmas Eve?"

"Obviously."

He bites the word out, and now that I have nothing to lose, I want to slap the expression off his face. Instead, I go for as much honesty as I can offer.

"Because sometimes you just need to escape from reality. And what better way than to let someone screw you into oblivion? And it'd been fourteen months since I'd been with anyone. I was overdue, and you were there.

I considered you my Christmas present to myself. That's how I justified it."

I turn again and reach for the handle as his arm wraps around my waist. It's the same move as when I was sitting on a bar stool downstairs. Before I can protest, he hauls me back against his hard, hot chest. I struggle, ready to elbow him to let go.

A harsh whisper in my ear doesn't still my movements.

"Fourteen months? You don't get to throw out something like that and then not explain yourself."

I continue to fight against his hold, and his arm pulls tighter.

"You're not leaving this room without giving me an explanation."

I can feel the ridge of his erection pressing against my lower back, and I'm battered with memories of Christmas Eve. I need to get out of here and *fast*, because I'm liable to do whatever he says. There's something about the man that I just can't stay immune to for long.

"I'll probably get sued if I tell you more," I say.

His hand spreads out across my stomach, his thumb sliding up and down beneath my breasts in another move I recognize all too well.

"I've got top-notch lawyers, Holly." His lips brush my ear, and heat gathers between my legs.

I have to get out of here. I tug again at his hold —unsuccessfully.

"Good for you," I say. "I hope you and your lawyers are very happy together."

His tone loses a fraction of its edge when he replies,

"They'll be your lawyers too, if you'd just explain yourself."

Those words finally still my struggle because they hit on the exact reason I chose him—my hope that he has enough power, leverage, and blood-sucking lawyers to uncoil the mess I've gotten myself into.

I took one leap of faith tonight, and I have no other alternatives. What is telling him really going to hurt now?

I suck in a deep breath before I whisper the truth that only the label execs, JC, Tana, and Mick know.

"My whole relationship with JC is a PR stunt organized by the record label, and I had no choice but to go along with it. JC and I . . . well, let's just say that we're both into male equipment."

It's as if I can feel the leashed anger drain out of him. He steps away, turns me back around to face him, and takes my coat from my hands, holding it up and open as if expecting me to slip my arms into it.

"*Now* you're throwing me out?" He really is the complete asshole his competition makes him out to be.

My thoughts are stolen straight from my head when, for the first time tonight, he smiles. And my panties are a lost cause.

"No, Holly. We're going to Vegas."

Holy. Shit.

CHAPTER FOURTEEN

HOLLY

I look down at the diamond on my left ring finger. You could buy the entire trailer park I grew up in with this thing, and still have money left over to buy a brand-new F-250 to park in front of it.

I lean against the plush leather of the limo delivering us back to Caesar's Palace, unable to believe I actually went through with it. I'm officially Mrs. Holly Karas, and tonight is my wedding night—or maybe to be more accurate, my wedding morning, as it's New Year's Day in Nevada now too.

I look at the man seated across from me. Creighton Karas.

I just married a billionaire. Granted, the prenup I read on the jet during our flight made it very clear that those billions are largely to remain his, regardless of the outcome of our marriage. If things fall apart, I'll have to refer to Section 39, subsections (a) to (zz), which list possible causes of the "dissolution" and the accompanying formula to calculate what I walk away from this union with.

Nearly fifty pages, and I read the entire thing. I was screwed by one contract, and I wasn't looking to get screwed by both this man *and* his contract. With my community college drop-out status, it isn't surprising that reading it mostly confused the crap out of me. If my adrenaline wasn't continually dumping into my system due to the looks Creighton kept giving me, I probably would have fallen asleep. Regardless, I'm guardedly confident that I understand enough to hope that I'm not missing anything obvious.

Creighton made a call to his lawyers as soon as we walked out of the twenty-four-hour wedding chapel. They now have their hands on a copy of my contract with Homegrown, courtesy of the e-mail I forwarded Creighton, and are going over it with a fine-tooth comb.

Apparently now that the task is in competent legal hands, he considers the matter handled. And for tonight, I don't think there is anything more I can do either. My phone has stayed off because I don't want to face the voice mails that surely wait for me. So instead, I focus on the present.

It's my wedding night.

Oh my God.

What the hell am I doing?

Aside from my one night with Creighton, I've been with exactly two other guys—my high school boyfriend, and a friend with benefits who was a regular at the bowling alley. With my high school boyfriend, I was lucky that he got it in the right hole on the first try. It hurt the first time, and all the times after that weren't a heck of a lot better. My friend with benefits was an improvement, but nothing like the night I had with Creighton.

Because of my prior lack of positive experience in the bedroom department, I've never considered myself a very sexual creature. Which is why agreeing to the label's crazy scheme with JC wasn't a huge problem in the beginning. But as the months wore on, something changed inside me. It probably has something to do with all the sexy books I read on the road while I'm touring. And the sinfully hot—and taken—man I'm touring with.

My Christmas Eve one-night stand was supposed to be just that—one night. And now I'm married to him. Every time I think about my current situation, I wonder if I'm crazy.

"You're awfully quiet over there, my darling wife," Creighton drawls.

"Please don't call me that if you're just trying to make fun of me." My voice sounds small, even to me.

His eyebrow lifts, and perfectly formed lips lift into a smirk. "Why would I make fun of you?"

"I don't know." I shake my head, trying to throw off his spell. "It's been a long day, and I'm still trying to catch up with everything that happened."

His playful expression fades, and I brace myself for whatever he's going to say next. Creighton's behavior hasn't exactly been warm and fuzzy so far, and his words have been decidedly no-bullshit.

"You don't need to catch up with anything except sleep for the rest of the night."

Shock courses through me. "We're not . . . I mean, you're not planning on . . ."

Goose bumps prickle my skin at his appraising look.

"The next time I fuck you, Holly, I want to make sure you're with me one hundred percent. I will accept nothing less than all of you, and right now your mind is a million miles away."

He's right. My thoughts are on the other side of the country, wondering what kind of hell I'm going to have to pay for this decision. And also a little at home, wondering if I'll end up on a bus back there if I fail to please my new husband.

I don't want to see this look of disappointment on his face. I want to see the heat that brought me almost to the edge of orgasm before I even followed his commands to strip naked. There's nothing I can do right now to deal with the fallout of the decision I've made, but I can try to make whatever we might have here work for both of us.

"Besides, I have all the time in the world to wring orgasm after orgasm from your body until your legs are so weak you can barely stand." His expression heats. "And plenty of time to train you to take my cock exactly the way I want—in every way, but first between those fuckable lips of yours."

All thoughts of anything but the forbidden things he offers are wiped from my mind. I want to see the approval I saw in his eyes that night, and that I heard in his voice when he opened the door at the Plaza. Something in his dominant nature snapped the pieces of my sexuality into place, and I want to revel in that feeling. Now.

I slide off the seat and drop to my knees.

Creighton stares down at me, and that dang eyebrow of his rises. "You praying, Holly?"

I shake my head. "No, sir. I'm taking your cock exactly the way you want it."

He doesn't miss a beat, just reaches up to press the limo's intercom button. "Keep driving until I tell you to stop."

Anticipation. Nerves. Excitement. And a unique and new sense of power. They're all flowing through my veins and controlling my actions.

Creighton settles into the seat and rests his big hands on his spread thighs. He's unreadable, but his words hide nothing. "I like having a wife who wants to suck my dick in a limo."

Shivers race across my skin, and my nipples pucker against the cups of my bra. Even though my body is screaming *yes*, I'm afraid I'll lose my nerve and look more ridiculous than I did before I started this.

"Would you please tell me to?"

He tilts his head to one side. "You are so fucking perfect." He reaches out and cups my jaw. "Holly, suck my cock until I come down your throat. Because even if I don't fuck you tonight, I want my wife sleeping with my cum inside her."

My inner muscles clench, and my panties are instantly soaked.

"Yes, sir."

"Good girl."

I reach for his belt and unfasten it before sliding

down his zipper. He lifts up and adjusts, allowing me to pull his boxer briefs down to free his cock.

If ever a man's penis deserved its own entrance music, it would be Creighton Karas's. It's long, thick, and perfectly veined. His heavy balls are already rising up to the base of his shaft.

I slide my hands up his thighs and lean forward. Pausing, I look up into Creighton's hooded eyes as I drag my tongue from base to crown. Salty precum beading at the tip urges me on. I make my first attempt at taking him in my mouth. On Christmas Eve, he whispered promises about fucking my face after he was sated with my pussy, but those promises never came to pass because of my stealthy early-morning departure.

But I'm going to give it my all now. I wrap my lips around his cock and suck him in. My progress is pathetic, but he shows no concern that I can't take him very deep. The stroking of his thumb along my jaw makes me want to try harder.

I adjust my position and take him as far as I can, gagging slightly on his length. He groans as I retreat. The tears streaking down my cheeks show just what a beginner I am at this. Creighton's thumbs wipe them away.

"Don't hurry it. It'll take time for you to get used to me."

Time. The one commodity he doesn't seem to waste much on women. But then again, he actually married me.

Regardless, his reassurance buoys my flagging confidence, and I take him further again and again, tongue working him over with each stroke. His groans of pleasure make me wetter and wetter until my legs are pressing together to soothe my ache.

I'm ready to climb on him in this fancy limo when he says, "Hold still, Holly. I'm going to fuck that pretty mouth of yours."

I still, and he guides my face to the most advantageous angle. And then his thrusts resume, picking up the pace until his rhythm slows and a wave of cum is unleashed in my mouth. I swallow as fast as I can, but I can't keep up. It dribbles down my chin.

When he finally pulls his softening cock from my mouth, his thumb catches the drips and paints my lips with them.

"Can't have my wife missing anything I give her."

The word *wife* is said with such possessiveness, I shiver and lick my lips. Reality sets in when he presses the intercom button on the ceiling.

"You can head back to the hotel now."

Creighton tucks himself into his pants and rights his clothing before I have the presence of mind to stumble back into my seat.

I can't believe I just did that. I push off the floor, intent on returning to my own side of the limo, but Creighton grips me by the upper arms and hauls me into his lap.

"Jesus, woman. You could wreck a man with that mouth."

His lips descend on mine before I can respond. His tongue delves into my mouth, fucking it just as surely as his cock had. I give myself over to the kiss, shocked that he'd kiss me after he just came in my mouth.

But he must not mind, because he doesn't pull back

until the limo slows and stops. When the door opens, he carefully sets me on the seat beside him, steps out, and reaches inside to lift me into the cradle of his arms.

My confusion must be branded across my features, because he says, "A bride doesn't cross the threshold except in the groom's arms."

I harden my heart against the erratic *thump-thump* his words produce. *It means nothing. It's a gesture of possession, just as surely as the ring on my finger is.*

As I tell myself these things, the exhaustion of the day sneaks up on me, and I rest my head against his shoulder.

I'll just close my eyes for a second, I think.

I'm out before we even reach the elevator.

CHAPTER FIFTEEN

CREIGHTON

"The country music world is reeling to learn that Holly Wix, a still-new addition to the scene who got her start on the show Country Dreams, married billionaire playboy Creighton Karas in Vegas last night. The couple was first photographed leaving an off-Strip wedding chapel, and then a short time later entering Caesar's Palace, where Karas is known to have a villa on reserve. When asked for a reaction, JC Hughes's representative responded with 'no comment.' Wix and Karas's representatives were unable to be reached. But we might as well acknowledge the question on everyone's mind: how long have Wix and Karas been sneaking around behind Hughes's back?"

I turn my head from the TV to the gorgeous woman passed out in my bed. In sleep, she looks even more innocent than she normally does. But she didn't look shy after she took my cock between her lips in the limo. It ranked as the top sexiest sight in my life, as well as a perfect way to kick off a new year.

My cock pulses at the thought. I picture myself waking her with my head between her legs. But for all that we're married, I'm guessing it would still freak her the fuck out. I'll give her until tomorrow.

My wife.

I didn't truly expect to go the marriage route again, but once I locked on the impulse, it was impossible to shake it. But even with a wedding ring on her finger, I know I won't get attached. I don't *ever* get attached. This is about continual repeat performances of the hottest sex I've ever had, and the added bonus of keeping the gold diggers off my back. Nothing more and nothing less.

My cell buzzes on the nightstand, and I grab it and head for the bathroom. Shutting the door, I glance down at the screen as I answer.

"What do you want, Cannon?"

"Holly Wix? You're the luckiest fucking bastard on the planet. You knew all along, didn't you? I mean, how could you not? Her face has been on TV enough lately that even I know what she looks like, and I hate country music. And then Jeanette doesn't stop talking about her and that cowboy-hat-wearing man of hers. I can't believe you didn't tell me, you fucking asshole. Had me and the rest of the world thinking you didn't have a clue who might show up last night. I should've known . . ."

I grit my teeth as he refers to JC Hughes as *her man.* Holly fucking belongs to me—not him. There's no disputing that as of the early hours of this morning. Even though I know the story behind it, I dislike the idea of another man thinking he has any right to lay claim to her.

Shifting, I lean against the granite countertop. Leave it to my second-in-command to jump to the conclusion that I actually knew who she was.

"And that's where you're wrong. When she's not covered head to toe in sequins, fringe, and ten pounds of makeup, she doesn't exactly look the same as she does on TV."

"Seriously? You really, truly had no idea?"

"None. At least, not until she told me."

"Holy fucking shit."

"Indeed." I'm already impatient with this conversation. "Anything else, or can I go about my morning?"

"Sorry. I'm still processing." Another moment of silence, and then Cannon asks, "Have you heard what the media is saying?"

"I only caught a few seconds of the news this morning. Why?"

"They're tearing her apart on every station, and all over the Internet. You should probably care that they're calling your wife a cheating whore. But then again, some of them are saying she made the right move because Hughes has apparently been fucking around on her since the beginning."

Rage burns through my veins, which might make me a hypocrite because I jumped to the same conclusion at first. But she's my wife, and that's fucking unacceptable. Holly said this would happen, and I told her I'd handle it. I'm not about to drop my end of the bargain.

"Get the PR team on it. Now. Crush anyone who says a negative word about her. I don't care what you have to do."

"How are you going to spin it?"

I fill him on the story I want fed to every major media outlet in the country—fuck, the world—and the accompanying threats.

Before we hang up, Cannon adds, "Since you're in Vegas, you should probably know that they're taking odds on how long this is going to last."

"They take odds on everything."

"Just saying. If you have any inside information, I'll happily go place my bet and rake in some easy money."

"Are you asking me to bet on when my marriage is going to end?"

"Come on, man. We all know this isn't going to last. So, what do you think? I give it six months at the outside before you're sick of her pussy and will be dying for some variety."

I grit my teeth because I don't have time for this shit right now. "Thank you for your vote of confidence."

"Seriously, Crey—"

"Fuck off, Cannon. Go fix shit."

I hang up, my morning mood turning dark as I open the bathroom door.

"How bad is it?"

Holly is sleep-rumpled and still wearing the undershirt I dressed her in last night after she passed out on me. Her legs and feet are bare, and her dark brown hair is tumbling down around her shoulders. She looks all of sixteen years old. Which apparently makes me a dirty old man, because I want that fresh-faced beauty staring up at me from her knees with my cock between her lips again.

"It's not good, but it'll be fine. Don't worry about it," I reply before asking, "How old are you?"

"You didn't google me?" Her eyebrows inch up toward her hairline.

"I prefer the truth, and not some shit made up on Wikipedia."

She looks down at her feet, and I almost miss her answer. "I'm twenty-two."

I'm too fucking shocked to school my expression. My eyes feel like they must be bulging from my head. I rub a hand down my face.

"Are you fucking serious?" I never considered she might be that young.

Her shoulders go back, and she straightens to her full height, a whopping five foot six or so. "If my age was important, maybe you should have asked me last night."

Holly has a point. Last night, I was so caught up in the hype of my own making that it didn't occur to me to ask. When she's wearing makeup and more than just my T-shirt, she easily looks several years older.

She narrows her eyes. "How old are you?"

"Thirty-three."

Her mouth forms an *O*. My morning wood rears up in my boxer briefs, and her attention drops to waist level.

A hesitant smile flits across her face. "Do you . . . um . . . want me to . . . ?"

She really might be the perfect woman.

"Get in the shower, Holly." I turn on the water in the palatial glass enclosure, but she doesn't make a move to strip.

The twelve showerheads begin to fill the room with steam. I hold open the glass door and wait. She still doesn't move.

"Are you waiting for an engraved invitation?"

She shakes her head. "I just thought I'd shower alone."

Ah. There it is. Holly's innate shyness that she can't hide. As much as I get a charge out of guiding her due to her inexperience, the sexiest submissive women I know are also some of the most confident I've ever met. I caught glimpses of Holly's confidence when she spoke about her career last night and the mess the record label pushed her into, and I'm determined to see if I can pull that from her when it comes to sex. An interesting and entertaining challenge.

My words are calculated to do just that.

"And I thought I'd fuck my wife in the shower."

Her eyes dart up to meet mine, spitting fire. "Is this how it's going to be? You say when, and I just spread my legs? Because I missed that subsection in your massive contract."

Ah, there we are. She has attitude, but she's untrained and needs guidance on how to channel it. And that's where I come in.

I cross the room and stop in front of her. "The only massive thing you need to worry about at this moment is my cock, sweetheart," I say. "And when and where I tell you to take it."

Her fist connects with my jaw, and my head snaps sideways.

Fuck. I guess I went a little too far. My new wife has way more attitude than I realized.

Rubbing two fingers across the surprisingly tender spot just below and to the left of my mouth, I study her. She's shaking her hand out and wincing.

"Damn, that hurts more than I remember," she whispers.

I'm intrigued by her reaction and her words. "I'm not sure whether I should be more surprised that you punched me, or that this apparently isn't the first time you've hit someone."

Holly peeks up at me from beneath long, dark lashes, as if the boldness of a moment ago has faded as fast as it flared up. She flexes her hand, and I don't like the pain telegraphed by her movements.

"Hold on."

I turn and leave the bathroom. My preferred villa at Caesar's is five thousand square feet, so it takes me a moment to load up ice from the freezer into a hand towel and bring it back to the bathroom.

Holly's seated at the vanity with her back to the mirror when I return, still flexing her hand. I crouch in front of her, and her eyes dart up to mine in surprise. I reach out to take her wrist, but she snatches her hand away.

"What are you—"

I wrap my hand around her forearm, pull her hand toward me so it rests on my knee, and press the ice to her knuckles.

"I would think it's obvious."

Confusion creases her features. "I would've thought you'd pull out the contract and point me to the section where it states there's an automatic annulment in this scenario."

My lips twitch at her statement. "I can't say that either I or my lawyers envisioned this one." My almost-smile fades away. "But don't do it again."

"Then don't say stuff like that to me." She jerks her hand, but my hold on her forearm is unrelenting.

"I think you'll find that I'll say plenty of stuff like that, and I'll only get more demanding and blunt." I swear I can hear her teeth grind. "What'd you really expect, Holly?"

"I have no idea. I must be absolutely insane to think I could do this." She laughs, and it echoes in the large master bath.

The sound causes my balls to tighten and my dick to go rock hard. There's something about this woman, and I don't have a fucking clue what it is, but my body responds to her like I'm Pavlov's fucking dog.

As she's sitting at approximately eye level, she doesn't miss my reaction. She looks up at me and back down to the tent in my boxer briefs.

"Ignore it."

"Um, easier said than done."

Once again, a smile creeps across my face, and I lift the ice from her knuckles. They're red, and a foreign thought invades my brain. I don't like her hurting, and especially not because of me.

"Don't do that again," I order her.

"Then maybe you should rethink how you speak to me," she counters before meeting my eyes again and adding, "I'm sorry, though. I probably shouldn't have done that. I just . . . reacted. Badly."

I set the ice on the vanity and rise. Crossing to the shower, I shut off the water and jerk my head toward the master bedroom.

"Let's talk."

CHAPTER SIXTEEN

HOLLY

I hit him.

Holy. Shit.

I *hit* him.

I haven't hit someone since I knocked Johnny Dagen on his ass for handing me five dollars and asking if that was enough to buy him a blow job because he heard that's what my mama charged. I broke his nose, and he never asked again. I was fifteen at the time. That wasn't the last time someone made me feel like a whore, but I certainly wasn't going to spend however long this marriage lasts being treated like one.

Burying memories of a past I'd love to forget, I follow Creighton out of the giant bathroom. Even though he brought me ice, I'm assuming this is when the annulment proceedings start.

I wish I never got out of bed this morning. I need a do-over.

Jesus. Why did I hit him? Something about his condescending tone just pushed me over the edge.

I woke up this morning worried about what the record execs and the media were going to say, and he brushes my concerns aside like they're nothing. And then I find out that he's eleven years older than me, and suddenly the decision I made seemed to take on a whole new level of cons I didn't anticipate. It's no excuse, but it's the only one I've got.

Creighton pulls on a pair of lounge pants—I have no idea where those came from—and settles into one of the chairs in the sitting room portion of the master suite. I take the chair opposite him.

"We need to lay out some ground rules."

I'm not sure I like the sound of that, because I assume what he really means is that it's time to lay out *Creighton's* rules.

But what did I really expect? That I'd have some sort of bargaining power here? My leverage disappeared when I signed on the dotted line.

I know it, and he knows it.

Then again, we both want something from the other, which I suppose puts us on sort of even footing. Except . . . not really. He has the billions and I just have *me*.

You can cover a girl with fancy makeup, false eyelashes, hair extensions, stage-worthy clothes, and strip off my extra ten pounds by starving me half to death, but it doesn't change who I am at heart. I'm still a girl from East Kentucky with big dreams and an even bigger fear of failure—because I don't want to go back to Gold Haven. There's nothing left there for me anymore, much to my gut-wrenching regret.

When I snap myself out of my impromptu trip down

my pothole-riddled memory lane, I find Creighton waiting, that damn eyebrow raised.

"Please, by all means, continue." My accent comes out stronger, and I blame it on my thoughts of home and the fact that if his rules have any impact on my career, we're going to have a problem.

He narrows his eyes. "Rule one: I like sex. I plan to have a lot of it. With you."

Well, then. The man certainly doesn't beat around the bush. "I got that one."

"If that's going to be a problem for you, my lawyers can—"

And there it is, the threat to end the marriage, which would put my career in jeopardy.

"End this marriage faster than it started?" I say quickly, interrupting him. "Because sex isn't a problem for me. I know what I signed up for. It's not like I think you married me because you found my conversational skills riveting. I just didn't realize I was going to be spreading my legs on command. I thought you'd at least, you know, pretend like I wasn't a whore. Although I guess that's all I really am. A really expensive whore."

Creighton's narrowed eyes turn absolutely molten. "Don't you fucking call yourself a whore."

"Then don't treat me like one."

We stare each other down, and I wait for his response. I'm expecting something along the lines of "I'll treat you however I want to treat you," but what I get instead is something completely unexpected.

"I'm sorry."

An apology?

"That wasn't well done of me. I may be a demanding asshole, but that's not exactly my style."

"Does that mean you don't want shower sex?" I'm pretty sure it's the slutty devil on my shoulder shoving these words into my mouth, because I certainly wasn't planning to say that.

Creighton's smile is lazy, predatory, and his eyes are hot and hard.

"I didn't say that, Holly. In fact, right now there's nothing I'd rather do more than walk you right back into that bathroom, strip you naked, and fuck you against the wall until you beg me to let you come."

My mind skips back to our first night together. It isn't lost on me that the man likes control. The last time we had sex that night, he toyed with me, refusing to let me come until I begged and pleaded—and then he *took* me. I've never had that before, and I was pretty sure I'd never have that again. Which was depressing to think about, because it was . . . amazing. My objection this morning wasn't to the sex, but to the way he spoke to me.

And with his apology, maybe there's hope for us yet.

I decide to take the first step, a peace offering, per se. I set the ice on the table beside me, stand, and snag the hem of my T-shirt. I pull it up and over my head, and drop it on the floor. Creighton's lips twitch into that sexy smirk I'm already starting to recognize.

"Then maybe we should postpone the rest of this conversation indefinitely?" I say.

"I like the sound of that."

I take one step toward the bathroom, and he says, "Stop."

I meet his eyes, and he holds out the shirt.

I look at it in confusion. "What?"

"Put it back on."

"I don't understand."

Creighton reaches for my hand, places the shirt in it, and curls my fingers around the soft cotton.

"I told you I was going to strip you naked and fuck you in the shower. I didn't say you were going to strip for me."

Seriously?

But I don't protest. I think it's the promise of the orgasms looming on the horizon, and the way he's looking at me with scorching heat in his eyes. Shaking out the shirt, I pull it back over my head and turn to head for the bathroom.

Creighton stalks me as I make my way back through the master suite into the crazy-nice bathroom. I pause in front of the huge glass shower enclosure and wait.

The heat radiating from his big body penetrates the thin cotton fabric I'm wearing, and I wait for whatever he's going to do next. The anticipation is almost a tangible thing.

His mouth must be only half an inch from my ear, because his breath ghosts along it when he says, "Get inside."

I open my mouth to protest, because I'm still wearing the shirt and underwear.

"Now, Holly."

The order sends shivers racing down my spine. Unlike before, his tone is smoothly seductive and commanding rather than condescending. It's intoxicating and impossible to ignore.

Stepping into the shower, I await his next command. I don't have to wait long.

"Turn on the water."

I reach for the fixture and twist. The hot spray hits me from several different angles, and I shut my eyes. Water soaks through the shirt in moments, and I realize that I'm giving Creighton his very own wet T-shirt show. And that knowledge is not unappealing.

When my nipples harden against the drenched fabric, I wipe the water away from my eyes and turn to face him. I want to see his expression.

He doesn't disappoint me. His eyes flash, and I'm treated to a wolfish smile.

"You like this, you dirty girl. Even though you rebelled against it, you like when I tell you what to do. I seem to remember you asking me to do that very thing in the limo last night."

I start to shake my head, but realize there's no point in denying it.

"I shouldn't like it."

"Fuck shouldn't," Creighton growls as he crosses to the shower, stripping off the lounge pants and boxer briefs. He wastes no time grabbing my soaked T-shirt by the hem and pulling it up over my head. It lands on the shower floor with a soggy *smack*.

His mouth drops to my nipple as his thumbs catch the

waist of my underwear. Without lifting his head, he drags them down my legs, and I kick them aside. He pulls away from my breast, his attention riveted on my mouth once more. He takes it. Takes *me.*

Cupping my butt, he lifts me off my feet. "Wrap your legs around me."

His erection presses hot, hard, and heavy between my legs. I shift my hips, loving the pressure of it against my clit.

He pulls back for only a moment. "Speak now or forever hold your peace, Mrs. Karas. Because otherwise, I'm going to fuck the hell out of you."

My nails dig into the solid muscles of his shoulders.

"Please. Now." They are the only words I can get out before he shifts and presses into me.

I've never been this turned on in my entire life. *Never.*

My eyes flutter shut, but I force them open as my body stretches almost painfully to accommodate Creighton's size. I want to see the ecstasy twisted in his features.

His thrusts come fast and hard, and the heat of his body is a delicious contrast to the cool tile at my back. Steam fills the air, mingling with my moans of pleasure.

At this angle, every thrust hits a perfect spot, and my orgasm builds with each bit of friction against my clit. I fight against the rising tension, knowing that the longer I wait, the more intense it's going to be.

Creighton readjusts to hold me up with one arm, and slips a hand between our bodies. The press of his thumb against my clit tears away any resolve I have to wait. I dig my nails into the tanned skin of his shoulders as the climax bursts through me.

My cry echoes through the enclosed space, and I swear I hear him laugh over the blood rushing in my ears. He continues to thrust, the pace increasing with each plunge, until my second orgasm is barreling down on me. My body clenches around him, greedy for every inch I can get.

"Fuuuck," he yells as he pounds home one . . . two . . . three more times.

His muscles flex and release until we're both shaking under the hot spray of the shower. His head drops forward, resting on the tile beside mine. My legs are locked around his waist, and I'm not sure I'll ever be able to move again. Not sure I ever *want* to move again. He pulls out before carefully lowering me, and I'm forced to disentangle my limbs from him and let his cock slip from my body.

"Jesus, woman." He tilts my face up toward his, both hands holding my cheeks. "You're fucking incredible."

And then his lips descend on mine once more, but they don't stay on my lips. They slide down to my chin, my neck, my breasts. Each nipple gets the attention of his teeth and tongue before he drops to his knees and worships my belly, and then my pussy.

I can still feel his cum leaking from my body, but that doesn't stop him from burying his face between my legs, nipping at my clit and delving inside. His hands clutch my rear, forcing me to use his face for balance. Which I have absolutely no problem with because pleasure is again sparking down my spine, and my knees are dangerously close to giving out.

But when the fingers of one hand skim down the crack of my ass, approaching my no-go zone, I squirm, trying to move away from him.

He tightens his grip, and my squirming is completely useless, except for how it moves me another notch toward orgasm. He went there *that night*, but I was too drunk on whiskey and pleasure to care or protest.

But now? In the broad and sober light of day? I'm not sure I can handle it.

He looks up, lust and confusion written across his features in equal measure.

"What? You have a problem with me eating your freshly fucked pussy?"

I shiver under his penetrating stare. It misses nothing. As if testing my reaction, those questing fingers lightly cross over the pucker of my ass again, and I try to pull away.

A grin curves his mouth into a devastating smile as he circles it with his thumb and adds the slightest pressure.

I flinch at the nerve endings rocketing to life. "I don't . . ."

He leaves that sensitive spot and I relax, but altogether too soon. He brings his fingers forward to dip inside me.

"You've never taken a cock up this gorgeous ass, Holly?"

My eyes widen, and I stammer, "No . . . no. Never."

"That's going to change." His flashing brown eyes are wicked when he adds, "Maybe not today—or even tomorrow—but when it does, I'll make you fucking love it. You'll beg for it."

I swallow as another flood of moisture drips onto his fingers.

"Don't pretend you don't like the idea, because your body has already spoken. Let me show you."

Shaking my head doesn't help because his questing fingers are already drawing my slickness to my back hole. My muscles twitch at the zings of pleasure.

Staring up at me, he presses one finger against my asshole. I try to remain unaffected, but it's a losing battle. I bite my lip to hold in my moan, but it escapes anyway.

"That's right, baby. I'm going to finger-fuck this tight little virgin asshole, and you're going to come on my face while I do it."

"Oh my God," I whisper as his touch tests and then breaches the ring of muscle. Tremors rip through me as his finger presses in.

"That's a good girl. You take it. You take everything I give you."

I don't remember moving my hands, but they're cupping my breasts and tugging at my nipples, desperate to spread sensations of pleasure.

His finger slides deeper and begins to thrust as his mouth lowers to my clit once again. The vibrations of his groans intensify the sensations rioting through my body. When I feel a second finger circling my entrance, I stiffen, but a nip to my clit distracts me from the flaring nerve endings.

My head thrashes from side to side against the cool tile wall, pain and pleasure mixing and sparking as he thrusts with his fingers and toys with my clit with his tongue, teeth, and lips.

This man owns every one of my senses, and I lose myself to his forbidden touches as he forces me higher and higher until I shatter.

CHAPTER SEVENTEEN

CREIGHTON

When I release Holly, she slides down the wall, her head dropping forward onto my shoulder. We're both on our knees under the pounding spray of the shower, and I wonder if every time I touch her I'll feel like I've found the goddamn Holy Grail. It's a little unnerving, and not at all a feeling I'm accustomed to.

I stand, carefully helping her to her feet. I wash us both and shut off the water before wrapping Holly in a giant fluffy robe. It swallows her small frame, and in her blissed-out postcoital state, she looks like a sated goddess.

I carry her to the bed and settle her on a mountain of down pillows. My chest tightens strangely at her sleepy smile, and I feel the need to beat on it like fucking King Kong. I am the opposite of sated. I'm revved, ready to fuck her into oblivion, and feeling like I'm the goddamn king of the world. Her orgasms fill me with this insane power trip, like I could tear down buildings with my bare hands and then reassemble them with only my willpower.

A light snore comes from the bed, and I glance over to her again. Her head lolls to the side in sleep, and her mouth is slightly open. I'm a horny bastard, and I can't wait to feed my dick between those lips again and watch her swallow everything I give her.

I think of the way her tight little ass clenched at my fingers, and I love knowing that I'm going to be the first man to sink my cock inside it. These possessive urges surprise the shit out of me. I don't get possessive, because I don't get attached. Ever.

I shove them all down, back to wherever they came from, and head to the shower to jack off.

CHAPTER
EIGHTEEN

HOLLY

W hen I wake up from my cat nap after the most amazing shower sex I've ever had— actually, the only shower sex I've ever had —I decide it's time to deal with the consequences of my New Year's Eve decision. The label has blown up my phone with calls and messages all day, and when I finally take Morty's call, I have to hold the phone away from my ear because his words are getting louder and louder, and more and more of them are curses.

"You fucked up everything, Wix! We had it all planned. We spent fucking money on this proposal to make it media-worthy, and then you were goddamn MIA. What the hell are you thinking marrying some fucking billionaire instead of toeing the line like I told you to? You don't get to make those decisions. I make the decisions."

When Morty finally takes a breath, I open my mouth to speak. But Jim must be on another extension or in the same conference room, because he breaks in.

"What's done is done. There's no going back now, and even if we could undo this Vegas farce, it'd be even worse. JC looks like an ass, but at least a heartbroken ass is sympathetic."

"She shouldn't have done anything in the first place! This is fucking ridiculous. I swear you did this just to piss me off!" Morty's yelled words are starting to hurt my ears.

"I told you I wouldn't fall in line," I finally say. "You didn't listen to me."

"You don't get to have an opinion, Wix. Your ass is going back to Kentucky!"

Jim breaks in again. "Come on, Morty. We talked about this. Sending her back to Kentucky isn't going to do anyone a damn bit of good."

For the first time since I answered the phone, a feeling of relief slides through me.

Morty grumbles, still unwilling to concede completely. "Well, she better fall in line from here on out." Finally addressing me again, he says, "You better not miss a show, a practice, a radio spot, a meet and greet, or even a frigging meeting, though, Wix. I will yank you off that tour so fast, your head will spin, and then you can go crawling back to your billionaire husband and remember the career you could've had."

"I won't miss anything. You have my word."

"I'll be checking up on every single thing. You see if I don't."

"I got it."

"Good. Now quit fucking up everything and go write

some goddamn songs for your next record. You still owe me six."

"Six? What are you talking about?"

"We're doing an exclusive for a big-box retailer. So go write some shit."

The relief I was feeling slips away, and I sink down into the chair behind me. "Six songs? By when?"

"You've got three weeks. I'm already setting up time for a songwriter to meet up with you in Dallas to try and knock some out. If you can't do it, then I'll pick something for you."

The thought of Morty picking songs for me was terrifying.

I can write, but six songs in three weeks? I try not to panic.

"Okay," I mumble. "I guess I better get started then."

"Damn right. Hope you weren't counting on a honeymoon."

Reeling, I shake my head, but he obviously can't see me. I start to reply, but the line goes silent. Glancing down at my phone, I can see he's ended the call.

Well, that went better and worse than I expected. I still have a career—unless I miss something, which I will *not* allow to happen. And I need to write six songs in three weeks. I haven't written anything in months. On top of the craziness of touring and this new marriage thing, I don't know how I'm going to get in my zone and find some inspiration. I guess I don't have a choice, so I'd better get started.

The door to the villa's office swings open and Creighton appears. "Do I need to crush them?"

His automatic support throws me for a loop, and warmth floods my veins. "Excuse me?"

"Do I need to crush your label?"

"Why would you do that?" I ask, stunned by the offer.

"Because no one fucks with what's mine. And that includes you."

The warmth dies away just as quickly as it came, along with the realization that I truly am just a possession to him. What did I really expect, though? Affection? I don't even know him. Which begs the question . . . will I ever truly know him? Or will this be over before I ever have the chance?

"We're heading back to New York today to meet with my legal team. They've reviewed your contract and are ready to make recommendations."

"That's not necessary. Morty and Jim aren't going to slap me with a breach-of-contract suit over this. And besides, I can't go back to New York; I need to be in Nashville. I have a life, you know. I have to check in with my manager and my band before we get back on the road again."

"That's not part of the plan, Holly."

"Considering you didn't consult me when you came up with this brilliant plan, you'll understand that I have a problem with it."

His eyes narrow, and his annoyance is clear in his tone. "How'd you manage to go to New York then, if you're on tour?"

"We had a break from Christmas Eve until after New Year's. We're back on the road on the sixth for the last leg of the tour. I need at least twenty-four hours in Nashville beforehand to get ready."

"Are you headlining this thing?"

"No," I reply slowly.

"Then why do you care so much about the tour?"

Is he for real?

I cross my arms over my chest. "Because this is my job. And apparently you don't know a whole hell of a lot about the music business if you think that I should be headlining tours at this stage."

"They can get a replacement while we work out our schedules."

I'm speechless for a moment. Is he really suggesting this? *Seriously?* I need to put this in words he'll understand without question.

"No way in hell, Karas. I'm doing the tour. Not only will the label definitely sue me if I miss a single practice, let alone a show, this is for the fans who bought tickets to see this show. I won't back out."

"Your fans can see you another time. The next few weeks are critical to figuring out how your career fits into the schedule so it doesn't interfere with mine."

I shove out of the chair and stand. He doesn't get it. This is the line I will not let him cross.

"Then I'm done," I say, confidence ringing in every word. I will not allow him to take this from me. I won't let *anyone* take this from me.

Creighton's brow wrinkles and he tilts his head. "Excuse me? I don't think I heard you correctly." He steps toward me.

"I said I'm done. I'm not disappointing the people

who support me to suit your strategy-session schedule, and I refuse to have my career dictated by yours. I should've known better. I bought your line of bullshit last night that you'd help me figure this out, not complicate it more."

The muscle ticks in his jaw, and his tone is deep and final. "And I said I'd support you, Holly. Not them. And my support requires that my business comes first."

"No. Let me put this in words you understand, Karas. This is a *deal breaker*. *Non-negotiable*."

I head for the door, and he steps into my path. "That's completely unacceptable. You're not done with me until I say you're done."

A laugh spills from my lips. "I'm glad you think you can just say the word and it's law. It doesn't work like that." I go to sidestep him, but he moves with me. "I'm not screwing around, Karas. I'm done."

I dart around him and make a break for the door.

Surprisingly, he doesn't stop me.

CHAPTER
NINETEEN

CREIGHTON

I f she thinks I'm going to let her walk out on me, she's insane. I let her get a few strides ahead of me before I follow her into the bedroom.

She searches the room, presumably to find the pile of clothes I folded neatly after I stripped her when we got to the hotel. Spotting them on the dresser, she grabs her jeans, and without bothering with panties, shoves one leg in at a time and tugs them up.

"You're not leaving."

Holly's head jerks up as she reaches out to grab her bra. Her eyes might as well be spitting flames for all the heat in them. "Watch me."

"That's not acceptable."

"You mentioned that already. But unfortunately, what you didn't mention was the only way this worked was for me to give up my career. To give up my *dreams*. You don't get it. My dreams are all I've got left, and I'm not giving them up for anyone."

I grit my teeth. This is why I was in no hurry to get

married again. Because women are completely fucking unreasonable and irrational.

"Then maybe you should have asked more questions before you agreed to this proposal."

She pauses after she hooks her bra. "I guess the only question I really needed to ask was whether you were a selfish, stubborn asshole. My mistake."

She's not wrong. I am a selfish, stubborn asshole. I wouldn't be where I am today without those qualities. But we also had a deal.

Holly shrugs on her shirt and tosses her hair back, plaiting it into a quick braid and securing it with some sort of elastic she pulled from the pocket of her jeans. Once again, she looks about sixteen years old, a defiant, gorgeous girl who just threw everything I can offer her back in my face because she thinks I'm going to make her give up her dream.

It's good to know one of us has principles.

"Sit your ass down, Holly. You're not going anywhere."

Her hands land on her hips and she glares at me. "You can go to hell, Creighton Karas, and take your damn prenup with you. You can keep the hundred dollars I'm probably entitled to after being married for twelve hours. Use it to buy yourself a blow job from some other clueless toy, because this one is *done*."

My smile sharpens because I actually like this feisty woman. I strike before she even registers that I'm moving. I toss her to the bed and pin her hands above her head.

"If you think I'm letting you walk away after that

display, you are sadly mistaken, my dear wife."

Her struggle is no pretense, and the knee that almost connects with my balls is also very real.

"Fuck you, Karas."

"Honey, the only one getting fucked here is you." I still her thrashing head by pressing my mouth to her ear. "Let me figure it out. If I can't handle something as simple as dealing with your tour and schedule, I'm not fit to run a multi-billion-dollar global company."

I can't believe I'm conceding this point, but I'm not willing to let her go. I will find a way to have it all, because that's all that I will accept. *Everything.*

Holly's struggling body calms as the fight drains from her. The only movement is the rise and fall of her chest as she sucks in lungfuls of air.

Her voice is quiet when she asks, "Are you serious? I need to hear you say it and mean it—that you'll make my career a priority too. Because for me, there's nothing more important. I need to be on that tour bus on the sixth, or I'm screwed."

I lift my head to meet her gaze. I'm not used to being questioned in anything, let alone whether my word is good.

"Yes, I will make your career a priority, and I will not be the reason you lose your shot at your dream. You'll be in Nashville by the night of the fourth—earlier than you said you needed to be there to get ready. But we'll do this all my way."

She studies my face for a long moment. "I don't get you. I really, really don't get you."

"You don't need to. And you probably never will."

CHAPTER
TWENTY

HOLLY

T he man is insane. That's the only explanation I have for any of this. And I guess that makes me just as insane because I've jumped on the crazy train right along with him. It's mind-blowing to think that so much has happened in less than twenty-four hours. At midnight last night I was meeting Creighton at the Plaza, we were married in Vegas this morning, and by mid-afternoon we're heading back to the airport for New York.

A bellman carries our bags as we leave Caesar's. The moment we hit the exit, cameras are flashing and reporters are shouting questions. I make sure my over-sized sunglasses are in place, and duck my head and hurry directly toward the open limo door just like I did the times the press caught me after another JC episode hit the papers. Without the limo, of course.

But before I reach it, Creighton grabs my hand and tugs me to a stop. He wraps an arm around me and pulls me against his side.

"Thank you for your felicitations. We'd be happy to answer a few questions."

We would? What the hell?

The press jumps on the invitation like vultures on road kill.

"Mr. Karas, can you confirm that this whole production—the viral missed connection—was a publicity stunt? And Mrs. Karas, can you address the rumors that JC Hughes was going to propose to you on New Year's Eve?"

Creighton shakes his head. "Now why would I confirm that? But I will say this. Sometimes to get what you want, you have to take a crazy chance and hope that fate is smiling down on you. This may not be the biggest gamble I've made, but I think it's going to turn out to be the best one. After all, I was the lucky bastard who got her to the altar first."

His words knock the breath from me. I look up at him through my tinted lenses and wish, in that moment, that I knew him well enough to know whether he's just spouting off crap for the press, or if he's being honest.

There's no way he really means it.

Creighton glances down at me, and a soft smile crosses his face as the flashes continue to bombard us. I know that picture will be the one on the cover of every rag tomorrow.

The press keeps firing questions, and Creighton answers them in vague generalities. He skillfully dodges the ones about JC, but he never looks away from me while he does it. I swear I hear the camerawoman directly in front of me sigh.

When we climb into the limo, I'm feeling very uncertain about this whole thing. My plan only included using Karas as leverage to free myself from the disaster with JC, along with the added bonus of having some phenomenal sex. But now that the wedding is over, I have no idea how this is going to work, despite his promise earlier.

I think part of my problem is that Creighton's motives are still a complete mystery to me. The sex can't be anything out of the ordinary for him, so is this all nothing more than a billionaire's whim?

But that look he's still giving me as we speed toward the airport, that soft one hinting at more going on behind the surface? What the hell is that? Is he still in acting mode?

And why do I care so much? I need to focus on my agenda and let him deal with his own crap. But that damn look . . .

"What?" I ask, unable to handle his scrutiny for another moment.

"What?" he replies with a shake of his head.

"You're staring at me."

His smile stays soft. "I'm faced with a beautiful woman. How could I not stare?"

"The press is gone, Karas. You can tell me the truth."

The smile dies, and I feel guilty that I'm the one who killed it.

"You're a bit of a firebrand," he says. "You know that, right?"

"I don't even know what that means."

His next words surprise me. "I think I'm going to like being married to you, Holly. And I think if you remove the stick from your ass for a few minutes, you might find that there's an upside to being married to me too. Life is short. We have to suck it dry while we can."

I ignore his fortune-cookie philosophy and say, "I do not have a stick up my ass."

"Well," he says with a chuckle, "I suppose I can personally attest to that."

Heat streaks up my body, and my cheeks flame. But even more than that, warmth flutters through my chest. It's like being in ninth grade and having the captain of the varsity football team tell you he likes-you likes you. I shouldn't care. I don't even know him. *And yet he's my husband.*

"You know what I mean, Holly. I get that you're protective of your career, but you need to unbend your spine a bit and settle in for the ride. You might find you'll enjoy where it takes you when I'm the one driving."

"I'm settled," I say.

"Sure you are, sweetheart. I think if I touched you right now, you'd bite off my hand."

The stupid fluttering in my chest gives me this insane impulse to bring back his smile. And prove him wrong. I wouldn't bite off anything if he touched me.

I unbuckle my seat belt, intent on changing this conversation the only way I've learned so far.

When I drop to my knees on the floor of the limo, Creighton surprises me by lifting me up by my armpits and depositing me sideways on his lap. "I appreciate the offer, but I'll take a rain check."

"But I thought—"

He presses a finger to my lips. "I think we're going to change this up, Holly. New rules."

"I don't like rules." The words come out garbled around his finger.

He smiles that freaking smile again. "And maybe that's the problem."

My confusion must show on my face, because his finger leaves my lips to smooth the space between my brows where my worry line always creases.

"We both know that you're a capable woman and your career means a lot to you."

I open my mouth to respond, but he presses that finger to it again before I can speak.

"Let me finish." He waits, and I nod. "I'm a dominant, take-no-shit kind of guy, and winning is incredibly important to me. When you get to my level, it's not about the money, it's about the win." He skims a thumb along my cheek. "I don't want to spend our time together fighting for supremacy, so here's my proposal: You let me lead. You don't fight me on every little thing, and you bend when I ask you to bend."

I feel my eyebrows inching up toward my hairline as he continues.

"And in return, I'll give you everything you could ever possibly want or need."

When his hand drops from my face, I take that as a sign that I'm now allowed to speak. "You mean, in exchange for my self-respect and free will."

Creighton shakes his head. "No. In exchange for your cooperation and trust."

"But—"

"Just give me a chance to show you what I mean, Holly. I don't want a docile little Barbie doll. I still want your spark and your fire. I don't want to tame it; I just want to guide it. And at the same time, I'll take every burden that's been weighing you down, and make them mine."

It's his last sentence that captures me—along with this rare glimpse of a side of Creighton Karas that few probably ever see. He's quite possibly the most capable man I've ever met, and the idea of turning my problems over to him is incredibly seductive. I can almost feel the stress begin to fade away at his words.

I look up into his dark brown eyes and give him the only possible answer.

"Okay."

CHAPTER
TWENTY-ONE

CREIGHTON

I'm going to own this woman—body, heart, and fucking soul.

CHAPTER TWENTY-TWO

My first act of complete trust in Creighton is boarding the jet without asking where we're going. He said he'll have me back in Nashville by the night of the fourth, and I'm going to take it on tentative faith that he will. A private jet should make that easy, I would hope. My plan is to get started on those songs I owe Monty, but Creighton has other ideas.

Once we're cruising at thirty thousand feet, he leads me into the bedroom that makes up the back section of the cabin, and says one word.

"Strip."

My first instinct is to argue, but with our newfound understanding at the forefront of my mind, I reach for the hem of my shirt and comply.

He reclines on the bed, fully dressed. Once I'm naked, I wait for his next instruction. I thank God that I'm not self-conscious as he lazily inspects my body. The ten months of being poked and prodded and changing in front of everyone and their mother—starting with the wardrobe consultants on *Country Dreams*—has pretty much stripped me of any modesty.

Finally he speaks. "I'm hungry, and I want your cunt on my face."

My heart stutters at his crude words, but my inner muscles clench with need. Maybe doing whatever Creighton tells me won't prove to be such a hardship.

I climb onto the bed, straddling him, and inch my way up to his face awkwardly. I've never just *sat* on someone's face before. But Creighton doesn't allow my hesitancy. He grips my ass cheeks with both hands, and I have flashbacks of this morning in the shower.

But any thoughts other than stomach-quivering pleasure are wiped from my mind when he tongues my clit and his mouth slides lower to feast.

I lean forward, grabbing the top of the upholstered headboard for balance. I cease to exist except in those places where his body touches mine. I'm mindless with pleasure when he finally latches onto my clit and sucks hard. A crushing orgasm rips through me. As I fall forward, Creighton twists so that I land on my back. He stands and tosses his pants and boxer briefs aside. He parts my legs and pulls me to the edge of the bed. Finally, his rigid erection presses into me.

Limp from the climax he just wrung from me, I can do nothing but grasp his shoulders and hold on while he pounds me into the mattress. Tremors ripple through me, and on their heels, another orgasm is spiraling out of control.

I have no idea how much time has passed when he

finally roars out his own orgasm and stills. It could have been thirty seconds or thirty minutes. My ability to comprehend the passage of time was lost to my capacity for pleasure.

He holds himself partially above me, our sweat mingling as his drips from his body onto mine. I decide, in that moment, that as long as he doesn't jeopardize my career, I'll follow his rules if he'll let me relive this experience over and over again.

And so my addiction to Creighton Karas begins.

CHAPTER
TWENTY-THREE

HOLLY

I've obviously been to New York before, but arriving on a private jet is completely different from arriving by tour bus or a commercial flight. Like the reverse of our trip to Las Vegas, we land at the private airfield, climb out onto the tarmac, and are met by a blacked-out, chauffeur-driven Bentley.

The short ride into Manhattan is uneventful, and Creighton is on his phone, responding to e-mails and things, and my presence seems to just fade away. But I'm not annoyed; I'm thinking too. I've got six songs to write and three weeks to do it. I have no idea what Creighton has planned for these couple of days in New York, but I'm going to sneak in a little writing time if I can.

Just as they did the first time I came to New York, the giant skyscrapers rising up from the concrete make me feel tiny in comparison. All the people bustling along the sidewalks—even at midnight, like now—move with purpose, intent on getting where they need to be. We slow in front of a tall building that's brightly lit, and I have no idea where we are in proximity to the Plaza, but I suppose it doesn't matter. The only part of the shiny gold address that registers with me is the large *Fifth Avenue* above the revolving glass doors.

Creighton tucks his phone away and pushes the limo's door open before climbing out and offering me a hand. I take it, wondering if we'll be walking into another media circus. Despite the late hour, cameras click and flash as we walk toward the doors, but this time Creighton doesn't even slow to acknowledge them. They don't come any closer, and I wonder why they're staying back, until I see security hovering in front of the building.

A doorman swings open the glass and gold door, and Creighton thanks him by name. The fact that he knows the man's name is a hugely positive sign in my book. An express elevator ride later, we walk into the penthouse, which comes as absolutely no surprise. It's huge, especially by New York standards.

Dark wood and some kind of fancy marble stretch out in front of us, covered by rugs that match the gray and white walls. But the centerpiece of the massive living room? The wall of windows looking out over the city. The view is amazing, even in the dark. It's very much a man's domain, though, overrun with black leather and glass. Splashes of color, mostly teal and red, are sparse, only in the artwork and a few pillows.

Overwhelmed, I hesitate, afraid to step inside with my boots on, but Creighton doesn't share my reluctance. He pulls me inside.

"You'll be comfortable here for a few days."

Again, it's not a question from him, but a decree. I can't argue with him. I'm sure the place has every creature comfort invented.

"It'll work," I say, and Creighton turns his head to smirk at me before leading me toward the bedroom.

"You're not wasting any time, are you," I mumble under my breath.

"Unfortunately, I have to leave you and go to the office for a few hours. Something came up, and I need to handle it from there with my team."

"You're making them work in the middle of the night? And on New Year's Day? That seems like cruel and unusual punishment."

Creighton pauses in front of the king-sized bed with a sleek black headboard and footboard, silvery-gray bedspread, and a pile of pillows.

"They work when I need them to work. No one comes on board who isn't willing to drop everything whenever I need them. The compensation they get is a fair trade."

I shrug. I've got no response to that, because I assume he pays them more than I make, so it's up to them what they put up with from him.

"Come. I want to show you your things."

"My things?"

I follow him toward a doorway that leads into a walk-in closet that's about half the size of the single-wide I grew up in. The size doesn't stop me in my tracks, but the collection of skirts, dresses, tops, and slacks hanging in it does. My eyes catch on the shelves of shoes, purses, and accessories.

"What's this?"

"Your wardrobe," Creighton replies matter-of-factly. "I had it delivered New Year's Eve."

What?

"On the flight to Vegas?" I'm so confused. When could he have done that? I don't remember him making a call, but then again I was buried in the prenup.

"No, before I went to the Plaza."

"That's crazy. You didn't even know if I'd show. Plus, it's kinda freaking creepy. I'm not some Stepford wife you can just dress up however you want."

Creighton's laugh fills the room. "If I wanted a Stepford wife, I would've picked one of the gold diggers out of the society crowd. You, my dear, are anything but. I knew that on Christmas Eve, and I know it now. If there's anything that doesn't suit your taste, it can be removed and replaced with something that's more to your liking. But I think you'll be surprised by some of the choices. Country chic, I think the consultant called it."

Once again, I'm stunned. I'm still trying to figure out how to respond when Creighton releases my hand and turns for the door.

"I hate to leave you on your own, but I have to go. Don't wait up for me, because it'll be late. If you get hungry, the fridge is stocked." He pauses at the doorway. "The bathroom is also stocked. I didn't know what you would like on that front, but the selection should be adequate. Shower and relax. I'll see you in the morning."

Apparently I'm only capable of nodding. Creighton's lips quirk into a smile, and then he's gone. I'm still making my way out of the bedroom when I hear the front door shut behind him.

Well, I guess that's that. I wander back out into the living room and pull my phone from my pocket. All my social-media notifications are still going bananas, so I ignore them, along with the missed calls and voice mails from a number I don't recognize.

It doesn't take a genius to figure out who would call me a dozen times and leave a dozen messages. I hope JC was right that no publicity is bad publicity.

Going to the window, I can't help but feel like Rapunzel staring down from her tower, although with much shorter hair. Except in Rapunzel's case, her tower was at least familiar. I'm completely out of my element here, and I've never felt every moment of my Kentucky upbringing quite so keenly as when I stand in this penthouse.

A lyric hits me almost instantly, and I squeeze my eyes closed and hear it again in my head. Pressing my forehead to the glass, I quiet my mind to everything but the words and melody that are taking shape.

Six songs. I need to write six songs, and maybe, just maybe, I've got the beginnings of one. My purse is still on my shoulder, and I hurry to the chair near the fireplace and pull out my notebook.

As I scribble out the words and notes, the thrill of excitement rises in my blood. I need a guitar. I really, really need a guitar. It's one thing Creighton couldn't know I'd want since he arranged for all of this to be delivered before he even knew who I was.

I look out the window at the darkened city. It's too

late to go exploring for a guitar now, so I keep scribbling lyrics, erasing them and rewriting, until my hand is cramped and my back aches.

I lay down my pencil and rise, my muscles protesting and my head fuzzy. The little sleep I got last night and the sheer craziness of what I've done is catching up with me.

Flipping my notebook shut, I wander back into the bedroom, hearing the siren's call of the giant bed. After running my hand along the silky-smooth comforter, I give up the battle and strip off my clothes where I stand before I slide between the covers.

Tomorrow. Tomorrow I'll find a guitar shop.

My eyes snap open and I blink several times, scanning the room.

Where am I?

Then everything comes rushing back. *Creighton's penthouse. New York City.* Turning my head to the side, I see nothing but smooth, unrumpled comforter beside me.

I sit up and stretch, my attention going to the clock. It's already close to noon, and there's no evidence Creighton ever made it to bed. Swinging my legs over the side and pushing off the plush mattress, I rise and survey the large bedroom.

Nope. No sign of him.

My stomach grumbles and I wander toward the kitchen, wondering if I'm going to find a note or something informing me as to where my husband is. The granite countertop is spotless and note-less.

I grab my phone from my purse, and see a text from almost three hours earlier.

I'll be home later. Make yourself comfortable. Call the doorman if you need anything.

I'm surprised he has my number, but there's no questioning who the message is from.

My burning desire for a guitar hasn't faded, but I have absolutely no intention of asking a doorman to fetch me one. This is New York, and New York has everything.

I pull out my phone to do some quick Google searching.

Bingo. Apparently Rudy's Music is a New York fixture, and looks absolutely perfect. I check the distance, and realize it's too far to walk. I have no idea how to get in touch with Creighton's driver, so I decide that for the first time in my life, I'm going to catch a cab. It can't be that hard.

I don't even bother to shower or change my clothes before I'm out the door. After all, I've got songs to write, and for the first time in months, I can't wait to dig in.

CHAPTER
TWENTY-FOUR

HOLLY

I'm riding high on the knowledge that I've just written the most epic song of my career to date. Granted, my official career has only spanned nine months, but I've been writing songs for much longer. Regardless, the song is epic. I'm as humble as the next girl, but even I know when I've struck gold.

I don't even realize the time as I walk through the giant door into the lobby of Creighton's building. For the last however many hours, I've been tucked into a corner at Rudy's, losing myself in the music. The super-cool old dude finally asked me to leave an hour after he would have normally closed. I guess he was caught up in the music too, but was gracious and awesome, and promised to come to my show the next time I performed in the city.

I swipe the key card the doorman gave me as I left the building, hit the *P* button, and lean back against the mirrored walls of the elevator. Because Creighton owns the entire top floor, the elevator opens directly into a lobby that has only one door. I left it unlocked, assuming only someone with the key card could get back up here.

I can't help but hum the melody of my new badass song to myself as I step into the darkened penthouse. Dropping my purse on the huge table in the entryway, I grip the notebook between my teeth as I tug off my boots. It's cold as heck outside, and even during the short walk from the corner where the cab dropped me off, I think I slogged through some nasty stuff hiding in the snow that has been falling since this afternoon. Since I take better care of these boots than some people do their children—they're one of very few extravagant purchases in my life—I whisper that I'll be back to wipe them off in a hot second.

I'm crossing into the living area and heading toward the kitchen when a lamp clicks on. The pooling light reveals Creighton seated in the chair by the fireplace.

For a moment, I'm reminded of one of those movies where the teenager is sneaking into the house after curfew, and the mom or dad is waiting in the living room all quiet-like before flipping on the lights and surprising the kid. Considering I never had a mom who cared enough about me to set a curfew—let alone ever have a dad—I've always been a little envious during those moments in movies. Gran was amazing, but she was in bed by nine every night, and I respected her too much to stay out past midnight, which was my self-imposed curfew.

Creighton's expression is dark, despite the crisp white light. "Where the fuck have you been?"

I stumble to a stop at the question. "Excuse me?"

"I said, where the fuck have you been?"

I'm taken aback by his tone. Creighton was the one who left within moments of depositing me in this penthouse, so if anyone has a right to be pissed, it would be me. And regardless of how nice a place it is, I'm not exactly the kind of girl who can sit idle. He never said anything about not being able to leave.

I try to interject some lightness into the mood. "It's lovely to see you too, my dear husband."

"Answer the question, Holly."

Seriously, why is he so pissed?

"I was out. I needed a guitar, so I went and found one."

"And you couldn't answer your goddamn phone?"

I glance in the direction of my purse. I don't remember it ringing, and I sure didn't look at it after I found my way to Rudy's. Then I look back to Creighton, a flare of guilt building inside me, but it's quickly doused when he pushes out of the chair and stalks toward me.

"You don't leave this building unless I know where you're going."

Say what now?

"Excuse me?"

"You heard me."

"I didn't realize I was a prisoner here."

"You're not a prisoner; you're my wife."

"Apparently that's the same thing," I mumble, dropping my gaze to the floor. Because I'm pretty sure if I look at him right now, I might incinerate him with the fire shooting from my eyes.

He lifts his hand, and I flinch before he cups my jaw

and lifts my chin. I'm forced to meet his gaze, and open my mouth to spit that same fire, when he says, "Scared the hell out of me to come home to find you gone. I came up with a million different scenarios while I was sitting here, calling your phone over and over. Thought maybe you'd run."

I blink, the intensity of his gaze unnerving me. "Run?"

"From me."

I bite my lip. A hint of vulnerability creeps over his features before they harden once more.

"Not that it'd do you any good. I'd track you down. There's nowhere you could hide from me."

My eyes widen at his words, and heat rushes through me at the sheer possession in them. I should hate it, but I don't. Being wanted is a feeling I'm not used to, and it's seductive.

"I'm not done with you," he finishes.

And the heat cools, because I can hear the unsaid "yet" floating in the air.

I clutch my notebook to my chest, trying to hide the pang that just jabbed at my heart. I shutter my expression, not wanting him to know that I feel the word he didn't say. Not wanting him to know that I care. Because I don't.

This is temporary, I tell myself. *We both know it. Embrace it. And then move on.*

"I guess it's handy that I'm not done with you yet, either," I say. It's the honest truth. I want more of him before he finally gives me my walking papers.

Creighton loses none of his intensity as he lifts his

other hand and frames my face. I think he's going to lower his mouth and kiss me, but he doesn't.

"Where the hell have you been?" he asks again, this time much more quietly.

Disappointment fills me. I was actually looking forward to that kiss.

"Holly."

I snap my attention back to him. "I told you, I needed a guitar. So I went and found one."

He drops his hands from my face, and I miss his touch as soon as it's gone. I should dwell on that, but I don't.

"Shit. I didn't even think about that."

"It's no big deal. I found this little music store. The guy there was awesome. He let me play for as long as I needed."

Creighton frowned. "You didn't buy one?"

I raised an eyebrow. "I don't need a new guitar. I have two perfectly good ones waiting for me in Nashville, and I'll be back there the day after tomorrow. The guy at Rudy's told me I could come back tomorrow and play if I want."

Creighton shakes his head. "You'll have a new one here tomorrow. Just pick it out, and I'll get someone to deliver it first thing. Your credit cards will be here too."

Both of these statements floor me. "I don't need a new guitar. And I don't need your money either."

His jaw sets, and his eyes drill into mine. "And yet you'll have both. This is not a debate. If you don't pick out a guitar, someone will pick one out for you."

"Are you ever anything less than completely stubborn and arrogant?"

Creighton's jaw relaxes as he smiles. "Never."

"I think you're way too used to getting everything you want." I say it without heat, because we both know it's the truth.

"Of course I am, and right now, I want you naked. I'm going to get that too."

And there go my panties. "Is that so?" I eye his three-piece suit. "Because you're certainly not naked."

He reaches for the knot of his tie and tugs it loose. "That's about to change."

Did I think my panties were a lost cause before? Because when he slides the tie from around his neck and wraps it around his fist, knuckles flexing, my nipples tighten.

"Lose the jeans, Holly. I want you bent over the back of the couch so I can fuck you."

My eyes go wide. I should be used to his bold state-ments by now, but I'm not. I'm not used to any of this. Not used to him.

He's . . . too much.

But that doesn't stop my hands from dropping to the fly of my jeans and unbuttoning them and dragging the zipper down. I shove them off my hips, and almost as if my body isn't under my own control, I kick them aside. My socks follow, and I walk toward the couch.

"The rest of it too."

My shirt and white cami are over my head and tossed to the floor in seconds, and I reach behind me for the clasp of my bra and it follows. I tuck my thumbs into the top of my underwear, about to shove them down, when he says, "Stop."

I freeze.

Creighton's presence is given away by the heat of his body as he steps within inches of me. I can feel him move, but I'm not sure what he's doing . . . until I feel his teeth against my ass, separated from my skin only by the fabric of my panties.

"I want a piece of this gorgeous ass. So fucking lush. So fucking tempting."

I remember what he said in the shower, and I tense. He reads my hesitation—I'm not sure how, but he does.

"Not like that, sweet girl. Soon. But not yet."

He tugs my underwear down my hips and presses his lips against the spot where he nipped me. His big hand skims up my ass to my lower back, and he pushes me forward. My breasts connect with the cool leather of the sofa, and I gasp at the contact. Which contact, I'm not entirely sure—but I can guess.

A groan from behind me has me lifting my head, but the pressure against my back keeps me otherwise in place.

"Jesus, Holly. That ass . . . I may have to fuck you like this every day."

Shivers course through me, and I can feel my arousal slicking down my thighs. Creighton's tongue zeroes in on it and he wastes no time lapping it up, his mouth working between my legs.

I shift uncomfortably. I've never done . . . this . . . from this angle, and he's getting dangerously close to the part of me that has never been touched by a tongue. But Creighton clearly doesn't share my discomfort.

I lift my ass higher in the air, pushing up onto my

tiptoes, trying to direct him without words to *keep his tongue the hell away from my back door*, and what do I get for my trouble?

A sharp slap stings the side of my rear.

"Ow!"

I can feel Creighton's lips moving between my legs when he says, "Stop squirming, Holly. If I want to lick this tight little asshole, you will not stop me." At the word *asshole*, his thumb presses against the sensitive pucker, which is already slick with my cream and his saliva.

A shiver runs through me at his words and actions.

"Goddamn, I love your ass," he says as he increases the pressure and the tip of his thumb breaches the tight ring of muscle.

My nipples? They could cut through bulletproof glass right about now. I shouldn't like this. I shouldn't want this. But God help me, I do.

And then he stands and steps away. As uncomfortable as the last few moments made me, I'm missing his touch already. I open my mouth to protest, but his lips press against my hair.

"Don't you fucking move. I'll turn that ass red if you're not in this exact position when I get back."

Okay, if I was turned on before, now I'm panting like a bitch in heat. And I'm no longer thinking I shouldn't want this. I don't care. I just want him to get his ass back here *now*.

I don't dare move a muscle, even though a part of me is sort of warming up to the idea of Creighton turning my ass red. *Where the hell are these thoughts coming from?* Oh yeah, my lady parts.

Creighton doesn't make me wait long. I don't even lift my head when I hear his footsteps crossing the living room. I might twitch a bit when he lays his big hand on the small of my back, but it's only because every contact with his skin lights up nerve endings I never knew I had.

"Good girl." His hand lifts and I relax, just in time for me to jump when a swat catches me just under the curve of my ass.

"What was that for?" My voice comes out in a hoarse squeak, and I'm not willing to even admit that sound can come from my body.

"Because I can."

I melt back into the couch. Jesus. This man.

Melting takes a back seat when I feel something cool and sticky coat the area that was previously designated as a no-go zone.

"Um, what are you doing?"

"Whatever I want. And it's just lube, sweet girl."

Uh . . . just lube? What the hell do we need lube for if we're not going *there* just yet? I don't voice my question because something is pressing against me there.

"What—"

"Hush," he says. "It's just a small plug. Not much bigger than my finger. I want to fuck you with your ass filled."

I suck in a breath. *Holy. Shit.*

But I don't protest. I don't think I have two functioning brain cells left to rub together at this point, because I'm a mess of nerves and physical reactions. Like the arousal coating my thighs and surely leaving slick spots on the back of the leather couch. But any concern over that leaves the building when the plug breaches the muscle and slips inside.

The breath I just sucked in heaves out of my lungs. He might claim that plug isn't much bigger than his finger, but he clearly doesn't get that in my ass, it feels *huge*.

"Oh my God," I whisper.

The slight burn subsides and it slips the rest of the way inside, anchored by the flared base. Creighton presses against it, and I shoot up onto my tiptoes.

A sharp smack lands on my ass, and Creighton's hand on my shoulder guides me back over the couch.

"Now we're ready."

I don't bother to agree, because his other hand is slipping between my legs to experience exactly how drenched his detour into *deflowering the back-door virgin territory* has gotten me.

He must have removed his clothes, because I feel nothing but hot skin and hard man pressing against me from behind. The hand on my shoulder slides up the nape of my neck and grips a handful of my hair.

The head of his cock slides along my entrance and I shift back, trying to help it slide inside. His smooth lips skimming along my earlobe are a counterpoint to his gruff words.

"You're never going to forget what I feel like inside you. I'm going to fuck you until you feel me with every step."

"Then what are you waiting for?" I whisper. I can't even believe I'm saying it, but I'm nearly mindless with need for him. I don't want to be teased, I just want him. Now.

"You naughty fucking girl," he says, dragging his teeth down the tendons of my neck.

I expect him to slam into me, but instead he presses in slowly, and I savor every inch as he gives it to me. I offhandedly realize that he's being thoughtful because of the . . . um . . . accessory he's introduced into this situation, which makes him feel even bigger than I remember.

Holy *wow*. Why don't guys with small packages insist their girls wear these? Or maybe it's only Creighton's generous equipment that feels impossibly large.

His careful handling of me doesn't last beyond the first few thrusts. It could be the moans that I can't keep from spilling from my lips. It could be the word *harder* that somehow finds its way into those moans. Regardless, Creighton's grip on my hair tightens, and he does exactly what he's promised—he ensures that I will *never* forget what he feels like inside me.

Thrust after thrust, he presses me into the couch, and his hand slides around my front and down to cover my clit. With every jolt forward, I feel his cock bottom out, and I buck against his hand.

"Holy fuck," I scream as my entire body begins to convulse with pleasure.

CHAPTER TWENTY-FIVE

CREIGHTON

Holly's pussy clamps down on my cock, and I swear to God, lightning is shooting down my spine. My balls spasm and I let loose, filling her with everything I've got, yelling the word *mine* when I come.

Fuck yell. I *roar*.

She's slumped over the couch, limbs unmoving. If it wasn't for the whimpering moans of pleasure, I might think I fucked her unconscious. Which I have no aversion to doing.

If her cunt strangling my cock is any measure, I think she came at least three times. Maybe more. It was everything I could do to not shoot my load after a half dozen strokes. Even without the butt plug, her pussy is tight, probably the tightest I've ever had.

And with that wicked addition, I succeeded in ruining myself for any other woman. No other pussy will do. I've said it before, and I'll say it again. This woman's cunt *owns* me.

Fuck that. This *woman* owns me.

I grab my boxer briefs off the floor, using them to catch the mess as I force myself to slide my dick out of her. I could happily stay inside her forever. Get me a phone with a never-ending battery life and I could do my business right here, while I give her the business.

God, I'm a fucking pervert.

I lift Holly off the couch and into my arms. Her head lolls against my chest, and her arms hang limp.

"Baby, you okay?"

"Mm-hmm."

"Let's get you in the bath and clean you up."

"Mm-hmm."

I chuckle at her languid response, and love that I'm the reason for it.

Settling her on the side of the tub, I flip on both faucets. Given that it's the size of a small pool, it'll take a while for it to fill. Without the insane water pressure I have, it would take an hour.

Crouching in front of her, I lift her chin and meet her still-dilated eyes. "You okay, babe? That was pretty intense." She nods silently. "Give me the words."

"I'm okay. I'm really, really . . . okay."

I smile at her response and rest a hand on her thigh, not far from the pussy that has me by the balls.

"You want me to take the plug out?"

A pretty pink blush covers her face, and her gaze drops away from mine as she shakes her head.

"Is that a no?" Another silent nod. "Words, Holly."

"No. I don't want you to take it out yet," she whispers to the floor.

My cock goes rock hard. Moments ago, I would have bet my jet that couldn't happen this fast. I would have been wrong—and flying commercial.

"And why's that?"

Her blush deepens when she replies, "Because I like it. And if I like that this much, I want to know what else I might . . . you know . . . like more. Which I'm assuming requires a little, um, prep? So yeah. That's why."

I feel her words in my dick and somewhere deep in my gut.

"Jesus Christ, Holly. You're fucking amazing."

I stand, scoop her back up, and settle us both in the partially filled tub. I keep her cradled in my arms, not wanting to let go of her yet. It's like I'm worried that somehow she'll slip away and I'll lose her—and that's not something I want to contemplate.

She leans her head against my chest, and I brush her hair away from her face so I can see her eyes. I don't know what I'm hoping to see in them, but I know I need this connection as much as I think she does.

This is a novel feeling for me. Even with the few longer-term relationships I've had, I've never felt like this. I knew she was something special; I wouldn't have done what I did and married her if I didn't think so. But it was a crazy-ass stunt I cooked up on the spur of the moment, and I would have never guessed I'd start to feel like . . . this.

Whatever the hell this is.

CHAPTER
TWENTY-SIX

HOLLY

I refuse to eat naked, and Creighton's narrowed gaze doesn't change my mind.

And so instead, I'm wearing his T-shirt and sitting in the middle of his dining room table. It's a very *Sixteen Candles* moment. I could swear I'm in the last scene, and I should be sitting on Jake Ryan's table with Samantha's birthday cake between us.

Except we don't have a birthday cake between us—we have enough sushi for a party of five—and I've just lost another kind of virginity tonight, because I've never eaten raw fish before. I figured, what the hell, I've already done something way more off the wall, so why not? And I'm glad I did, because it was *a-maz-ing*.

I'm a total klutz with chopsticks, so I give up and pick up the piece of something Creighton called a rainbow roll and dip it into soy sauce mixed with a small bump of wasabi. I hold my hand under it to catch the drips as I lift it to my mouth, already anticipating the symphony of flavors I'm about to unleash.

Creighton's smile is downright amused, but I don't care. He might as well see how completely unsophisticated I still am in so many ways. At least he won't expect to take me out to some fancy restaurant until I've had time to master chopsticks. It's not like we used them to eat hot wings at the bowling alley.

I moan in delight as I savor the taste of the sushi I've just popped into my mouth. It's so damn good, and I say so to Creighton as soon as my mouth isn't stuffed full.

"I'm glad you're enjoying it."

"I can't believe I never wanted to try it before. If I'd only known what I was missing . . ."

"I'm glad you're open to trying new things, Holly." His lips twitch into a less amused smile. "I can't wait to see what we can conquer next."

I lift my sweet tea, procured by Creighton at my request, to take a sip. "It'll have to wait until after the tour." I note Creighton's frown and add, "You didn't forget that, right?"

"No, but I forgot to tell the pilot."

Oh, that's not a good sign. "Maybe you should do that?"

He shoves a hand through his hair and slides off the table. I'm hoping he's taking care of the situation, and in the meantime I watch the play of the muscles in his back, all the way down the waistband of his gym shorts, as he crosses the dining room and disappears into the kitchen. His voice carries, and I'm pleased to hear he's making the call.

I pick up his half of the conversation.

"This is Karas. I'll need the jet the day after tomorrow. Make sure it's ready by four."

"Good. Text me if anything comes up in preflight."

"Thanks."

I'm feeling the warm glow of contentment that he's making sure I'm going to get back to Nashville early when he heads back into the dining room and climbs back onto the table. But not on his side. He settles himself behind me, lifting me so I sit on his lap.

"We're going to teach you to eat with chopsticks."

"This is going to get messier than it already is, then."

"So be it." He grabs the chopsticks with his left hand and places them in my right hand, positioning my fingers awkwardly around them. "Like this."

He guides my chopstick-holding hand to the sushi and manipulates my fingers until we've picked up a piece and dipped it in soy sauce. Ever so carefully, we lift it toward my mouth. Which is right about when I realize what we're doing is almost more intimate than when he bent me over the back of the couch.

My hand shakes, and the chopsticks lose their light grip right before it reaches my lips . . . and the cold rice and fish slips right down the neck of the T-shirt I'm wearing.

"Damn it," I say. "I knew this was going to be a disaster."

Sushi might be delicious, but it feels kinda gross now that the rice is stuck to my boobs and the fish is some-where farther south, near my own tuna.

Creighton chuckles before reaching his hand down the neck of the shirt and scooping up the remains. I twist and watch as he pops it into his mouth.

"Tastes even better."

I slip my hand under the shirt and grab the errant piece of fish, holding it between a thumb and forefinger. He nips my fingers before snatching it up.

"How about we skip the chopsticks? I'm lucky if I can figure out which fork to use. Adding in completely new utensils isn't really fair for this Kentucky girl." I lean back against him, the novelty of this position not yet wearing off.

"Tell me about it."

His question confuses me. "Tell you about what?"

"Being a Kentucky girl."

I twist again to take in his expression. He looks genuinely curious, but that doesn't really make me want to share. My upbringing was light years away from anything Creighton can imagine.

"Nothing much to tell."

"Now, that I don't believe."

I think about what I can tell him.

I was born in a tiny town with one red blinking light. I'm not even sure that qualifies as a one-stoplight town. I never knew my father, probably because my mama wasn't so sure who he was either. My earliest memory was stuffing all my toys and clothes in a garbage bag and dragging it behind me as we moved from trailer to trailer through the park as she hooked up with loser after loser. Paper-thin walls didn't muffle the sound of her "earning" our keep.

I took refuge in music—putting my headphones on and turning up the volume to drown it all out. One of the least loser-ish of the losers gave me a hand-me-down iPod loaded with tons of country music. Living in

Kentucky, that's about all I heard anyway, but he had the classics too. Loretta Lynn, old Reba, the Man in Black—I soaked up their words and eventually started writing my own.

When I was fourteen, my mama hooked up with a man who had enough money to buy her a Cadillac Eldorado, but didn't want to have anything to do with a kid. She clutched the keys to her new Eldo in her hand as she told me to pack my bags, because I was moving in with my gran.

Doing what I've done so many times before, I loaded everything I owned into a garbage bag and stuffed it in the trunk of the Eldo. My one and only ride in that car was across the river, where she dropped me off like a litter of unwanted kittens. I suppose I should be lucky she didn't stop at the bridge and attempt to drown me. Gran lived a half mile from the happening hot spot in town: Pints and Pins, affectionately known as Brews and Balls by the locals.

But I couldn't tell him most any of that. I decide on the streamlined version.

"I'm from a one-stoplight town. My gran raised me after my mama decided to do some exploring. It was better that way, because Mama bounced us around a lot, depending on what guy she was . . . dating at the time. I worked at a bowling alley to help make extra money."

My gran and Brews and Balls were both my salvation in different ways. Gran because she welcomed me with open arms and gave me the unconditional love and stability I lacked for the first fourteen years of my life. Birthday cakes, Christmas presents—those things became expected instead of the hit-or-miss mess they were with my mama.

When he doesn't speak, I continue to fill the silence. "Gran lived on Social Security, so every extra dollar helped."

To myself I add, *Because my mama sure didn't send any home*. Nope, after she packed up her Eldo and hooked it to the back of the rich man's motorhome and rode out of town, we didn't hear from her for years.

Shaking off the bitterness, I kept going. "Brews and Balls was the first stage I ever stood on to sing in front of people. One karaoke night, the crowd wasn't getting into it, so Benny, the owner, decided to take matters into his own hands. He'd heard me singing to myself in the kitchen while I was frying up onion rings and hot wings and chicken fingers, and decided that I'd do just fine. He pushed me out of the kitchen and into the bar, not even giving me time to drop my apron. The song was 'Born to Fly' by Sara Evans. When I finished, there was dead silence . . . and then the crowd went crazy."

I close my eyes, the memory still vivid in my head. When I stepped off the stage, Benny had tears in his eyes. *"You surely were born to fly, Holly."* He was the first and only man ever to believe in me.

And wouldn't he just be proud of me now? Mostly naked with a butt plug up my ass, sitting on this man's lap who I married after spending a single night with him.

I push the thought away. I'm going back to Tennessee in less than forty-eight hours. Back to normal. Which was a crazy thought all by itself—that my normal is life on a tour bus, heading out to sing in front of crowds of thousands in stadiums across the country. That's what I need to focus on, not the man whose chest I'm pressed against and the awkward silence I'm just now realizing has overtaken the room.

"How'd you go from karaoke in a bar to touring?"

"Benny pushed me to try out for *Country Dreams*, and when I got past the initial audition, I decided I couldn't go because Gran's health was getting rocky. I couldn't leave her, and we couldn't afford in-home care. But somehow, through the grapevine, my mama heard about the show and that I was going to turn it down, and she showed up on Gran's doorstep the day before I needed to report to Nashville for filming. She promised she'd take care of Gran if I'd only just take this shot."

I swallow, the lump in my throat growing. The last part of this story is the hardest, and the reason for the guilt that tugs at my soul on a regular basis.

"When the finals came around and I made the cut, my mama decided Gran could take care of herself, so she left her. She just wanted to be on TV when they showed my family in the audience, and meet some famous people." I pause, my heart clenching at the memory. "But Gran fell and hit her head, and never woke up again. She died before I could make it home to even sit by her bedside."

"I'm so sorry," he starts, but all the emotions and memories are bursting through my walls, and I can't stop.

"You want to know what it's like to wish I'd never taken a shot at my dream because my selfishness—and my idiot move to trust my mama—was responsible for the death of the only person who ever really cared about me?"

"Holly—"

"Or that I've been ignoring dozens of missed calls and messages that I know are from her because she's probably seen the news, and the only reason she'd be calling is for money?"

His arms wrap around me and squeeze me tight. "Holly, slow down. Breathe."

His words highlight the fact that I'm breathing so fast, I'm liable to hyperventilate. Creighton rubs my back as I force myself to slow my breaths until my chest rises and falls in time with his.

Crap. I can't believe I just spilled all of that. I've officially shattered any illusion that Creighton might have had about my background.

I pull away from him and stumble off the table. My soul is shredded with the telling of it, and I'm too raw to face him and his questions any longer.

"I think I've had enough sushi tonight. I need a shower to clean up now too."

I don't look him in the eye, and I don't wait for a response. I turn on my heel and head for the bathroom.

His ominous words follow me inside. "This conversation isn't over."

CHAPTER
TWENTY-SEVEN

CREIGHTON

I'm naked in bed, waiting for Holly, when I hear her voice coming from the bathroom. She's singing. Even though it's muffled by the water, glass, and walls between us, I can tell it's heartbroken and haunting. I didn't plan on that kind of emotional baggage from someone so young, but it's impossible to ignore. She's not broken, but she thinks she is.

The sound of her voice has me on my feet and crossing the room to stand in the bathroom doorway.

Steam fills the shower enclosure, but I can see her clearly enough to watch her rinse the shampoo from her hair. As the suds slide down her body, her voice grows quiet before she stops. I wonder if she realizes that I'm watching, but instead she presses both hands to the tile shower wall and leans forward.

In that moment, I know the water is drowning her tears, and I feel an urge I've never felt directed toward someone who wasn't family: the urge to comfort. I dried my little sister's tears once upon a time, but I never expected that another woman's would affect me so acutely.

I want to walk into the shower and pull her into my arms, but I have a gut feeling that she wouldn't welcome the knowledge that I'm seeing her at her weakest. Holly may be submissive sexually, but her inner fire and spark is driven by pride that I realize mirrors my own. She's young, but she's lived a hard life already.

I have the inexplicable desire to make it easy for her. To wash away the guilt and hurt in a way the water never will. But I don't know how to do that. It's something even my money can't buy. And the very fact that I wish I could scares the fucking hell out of me in the way I've never experienced.

What is she doing to me? I want to own her, keep her, ensure that she's mine, but I didn't expect to feel like . . . like this. The intensity of my need would scare the shit out of her too.

I turn away when she pushes off the wall and reaches for the shower control to turn the water off. By the time she leaves the bathroom, I'm back in bed with a myriad of possible things to say running through my mind.

But every single thought flies from my brain when she walks into the bedroom, wet and naked.

Fuck, but the woman's body is downright sinful. Full tits, small waist, flared hips, toned legs. Even as all of the blood in my brain rushes directly to my cock, I have enough brain cells firing to appreciate that she's more than a traffic-stopping body. She also has invisible scars and insecurities that I need a map to navigate without triggering. I'm starting to comprehend the enormity of what I've undertaken when I said, "I do."

She stops, and her teeth dig into her lower lip.

I wait, curious to see what she's going to say. With Holly, I never really know—and I'm finding I like that unknown.

"Can you ... help me out?"

I almost say that I'll help her with any fucking thing she wants, but I don't. "With what?"

She bites her lower lip again and lets it slide between her teeth. "With, um, the plug?"

A small smile curves my lips. "You didn't take it out in the shower?"

A short, jerky shake of her head is her only answer.

"And why's that, Holly?"

Her gaze drops to the floor, which won't do. Sliding back into the roles that we've carved out is easier for me than addressing the events of tonight, and maybe that's exactly what it takes to bring back the Holly I'm already addicted to.

"Look at me when you answer me."

A blush I'm becoming more and more familiar with stains her cheeks as she lifts her gaze to mine once more.

"I thought since ... you know, you put it in, that you should be the one to, um, take it out."

She's perfect.

"Good girl. If you'd taken it out without my permission, I would've had to spank that pretty ass."

I toss the covers aside, swing my legs over the edge of the bed, and stand. Her attention immediately falls to my dick. I don't correct her, because I like her attention there. She'll be paying it a whole hell of a lot more attention in a few minutes. But first . . .

"Turn around and bend over."

Her blush turns from a luscious pink to a fiery red.

"Excuse me?"

"Do I need to repeat myself? Because if so, your ass is going to be as red as your cheeks, sweet girl."

Her throat works as she swallows. I open my mouth to repeat my command, but she spins on her heel and bends over before I can get out the words.

My hand flexes with the need to smack that heart-shaped ass. I don't want to confuse her, but I can't resist. I pull back and deliver a stinging slap just under the curve of her right ass cheek. She inhales sharply and starts to rise, but my hand at the small of her back holds her in position.

"Don't move."

"But—but why?"

I crouch and trail my hand down the side of her body, stopping to cup her breast and roll her nipple between my thumb and forefinger.

"Because I can, Holly. Because your body belongs to me. And because you want it."

A shiver races through her and her nipple stiffens further, confirming my words.

I release my hold on her nipple and drop my hand to the back of her calf. I rise slowly as I drag my palm up the back of her leg to her ass. I find the base of the plug with my thumb and press against it.

I'm rewarded with another harsh intake of breath.

"I'm taking it out, but a bigger one is going back in

tomorrow. I don't have a lot of patience, and I can't wait much longer to fuck this gorgeous ass." I pull the plug out by the base and fuck her with it a few times before withdrawing it completely.

I turn toward the bathroom, but pause to tell her, "Be on your knees when I come back out. I'm going to fuck your mouth before we go to bed."

She shivers visibly. *My dirty girl.*

I take care of the plug in the bathroom and return to find her waiting on her knees . . . just missing the mark of obedient because her hand is between her legs, and her eyes are closed as she rides out an orgasm.

I watch—raptly—because Holly in the throes of climax is the hottest fucking sight on the goddamn planet. But my enjoyment in watching her doesn't mean I won't enjoy punishing her even more.

"Couldn't wait for me, I see."

Her eyes snap open, and if it's possible, her cheeks turn even redder. "I . . . I needed—"

"You needed to wait and take what I give you. And since you've already gotten yourself off, I guess that means you don't need me to eat that pretty pussy until you're so drunk off the pleasure, you can't move."

Crestfallen. That's the word that perfectly describes her expression.

"But—"

"Keep that mouth open, baby, because you're about to take my cock down that gorgeous throat of yours."

Her jaw drops, and I smile.

"Perfect." I step toward her, cupping her chin and running a thumb along her lower lip. "Fucking perfect."

My cock is straining up toward my navel, so I grip the base and bring it to her lips. Her tongue slips out and flicks the head.

"Grab my ass with both hands. I want you in position, and I don't want you tempted to fuck yourself with your fingers."

She complies, and I feed my cock into her mouth. She takes more than she did the last time, and I know this won't last long. I bump the back of her throat, and she gags a little.

"Swallow me, baby. I want to feel your throat work me."

Again, she complies, and I begin to thrust. In and out, reveling in the hot, wet heaven of her mouth. She takes me like a champ, her little moans sending out vibrations I can feel in my balls.

I have the primitive urge to mark her as mine. I feel my sac tighten, and I decide I'll finish on her tits next time.

"Ready, baby?"

She nods, and her nails dig into the muscles of my ass. I fucking love it.

My orgasm shoots down from my spine, and she swallows every drop that I give her. She's the perfect fucking woman. The perfect fucking *wife*.

I help her off her knees after I'm finished, and wipe the edges of her mouth with my thumb.

"You're a fucking goddess, Holly."

Her answering smile is shy as I back her toward the bed. When the back of her legs touch the mattress, she sits, and I drop to my knees.

"And it's my turn to worship."

And worship, I do. Until she's come three times, and I can still feel the marks her nails left in my scalp as I settle into bed and wrap myself around her, tucking my once-again hard cock between her ass cheeks.

As I'm dozing off, one hand cupping a breast, I wonder if I'll ever be sated with her.

CHAPTER TWENTY-EIGHT

HOLLY

Something about last night—the sushi, sitting on the table, telling Creighton about my past and the intimacy we shared after—trips my brain into a whole new side of married life. I'm afraid to trust it, afraid to rely on it. Skepticism is one quality I've got in spades.

So when I open my eyes the next morning, expecting to see an empty space in the bed beside me and yet Creighton is there, a tiny bit of that skepticism fades away. Maybe I am a little bit important to him. I thought for sure he'd be off running an empire right now, leaving me alone again at the earliest possible moment. His presence provides some hint of validation that I don't want to admit needing.

As these thoughts roll through my brain, I realize it's only the second time I've seen him asleep, the first being the early hours of Christmas morning. But that morning, I only chanced a glance at him before I hurriedly shoved all my stuff in my bag and tiptoed to the door. He was supposed to be nothing more than a way to forget that I'll never share another Christmas Eve with Gran . . . and yet now he's my husband.

Face relaxed in sleep, he looks younger than his thirty-three years. Without that blinding intensity and those piercing eyes focused on me, I'm able to study him at my leisure. Dynamic. Ruthless. Driven. Those are three words I'd use to describe him. Even in sleep, he's probably dreaming about conquering something.

I know I should wonder about his motivations behind this whole marriage, but I find that I don't care. Whatever it was that sent him on this wild hair, I should find it in me to be grateful. Otherwise, I'd be wearing another man's ring and living an even bigger farce.

Glancing down at the ring on my finger, I realize that I like it there. Warmth creeps into my veins at the sense of belonging I feel.

Crap. I'm starting to get attached. Danger!

The terrifying realization is interrupted when Creighton's eyes flick open and his gaze lands on me.

"Are you watching me sleep?"

I decide to go with the truth. "Yes."

His lips curve up, and I catch a flash of his white teeth. I think it's a genuine smile, but they're so rare for him, I have to actually think about it.

When he stretches his arms overhead and the sheet falls away, his washboard abs rippling, I forget about the smile completely. How can a man who sits at a desk all day look like *that*?

My mouth opens before I can engage my brain. "Do

you leave your desk to climb buildings or something? Seriously, those aren't desk-jockey abs."

His smile shifts into the smirk I've become very familiar with as his gaze jumps to mine.

"You're saying you actually like something about me?"

Creighton's eyebrow goes up, and I know he's having fun with me, so I give it back to him.

"I'm saying I'd like those abs on any man, so I guess I'm lucky they're yours."

His eyes narrow at my words. "Any man?"

His tone is quiet and even more intimidating than normal. I have only that tone as the slightest warning before he rolls and reaches for me. My squeak of surprise fills the room as he draws me closer and pins me beneath him, one forearm on either side of my head.

"There are no other men when it comes to you, do you understand me, Holly? None. You belong to me."

Whoa. Holy possessive alpha-male alert, Batman.

I push up on my elbows, bringing my lips within a breath of his. "As long as that means there aren't any other women for you, then we have a deal."

"You think you can bargain with me?" Every movement of his lips brushes them across mine.

"I'm sure going to try," I reply, my daring knowing no limits this morning.

"Sassy girl. You know that just makes me want to teach you a lesson, right?" His tone is a low growl, and his lips continue to tease mine with the hint of a kiss.

Untangling one of my arms from beneath me, I reach up and bury my fingers in his dark hair. "Then what are you waiting for?"

His lips crash down against mine, and words cease to be necessary.

———

Creighton leaves the penthouse to head to work around ten a.m., and when he promises that he'll be back to get me by seven, I actually believe him. Maybe it's the look in his eye when he left the bed that clearly said he didn't want to leave me there alone. It's like something finally clicked, and like a train, we've shifted onto a different track. One where maybe we can figure out how to coexist peacefully.

When I finally drag myself out of bed, I shower and breeze through my morning routine, dressing in some of the most casual of the new clothes in my closet. Glancing at the TV, I think about turning it on, but really don't want to know if my marriage to this complicated man is still the top story.

Creighton promised days ago that if I just trust him, he'll take care of the press side of things, and I shouldn't worry because it's a pointless waste of energy. I decided he was right and just buried my head in the sand. If a billionaire can't stop them from saying what they're going to say, how can I? It's wasted effort.

A voice calls out from the entryway, distracting me from my thoughts.

"Mrs. Karas? We have a delivery for you at the request of Mr. Karas."

Mrs. Karas? It sounds so foreign that it takes a moment before I realize whoever is here is looking for *me.* I look down at my gray long-sleeved thermal and black leggings, and wonder if I should run back into the bathroom and lock the door.

Screw it. I am what I am, and that's all I'm going to be.

I leave the bedroom and head into the living room. Whoever it is didn't come in and make himself at home, so I continue into the entryway. A uniformed doorman stands just inside the door, looking slightly uncomfortable as he holds a large rectangular box.

"Oh, excellent, I was afraid I might have entered at an inopportune time," he says, holding out the box in my direction. "Mr. Karas specifically requested that I bring this inside when it arrived. Where would you like me to put it?"

What in the world?

"What is it?" The question pops out before I have a chance to think.

He smiles kindly, but with a lopsided tilt that you'd give a clumsy puppy or small child. "I don't know, ma'am. You'll have to open it and see. Where would you like me to put it?"

Duh. Of course he doesn't know.

"On the . . . coffee table is fine." I point to the living room as I stammer over my words. I almost said dining room table, but even the thought of it reminds me of what we did on that table last night, and it seems obscene.

I realize too late that maybe I should have tipped the doorman, but he's already out the door and I'm left alone with the box.

Cautiously, I study it like it might contain human

body parts, because that's how I think in terms of measurement.

Trunks of cars? How many bodies can you fit in there?

Chest freezers? Same thing.

Creepy, right? Maybe I was a serial killer in another life, but I'm hoping not. Hopefully it's just a country thing.

I use my fingernails to peel back the tape and tear the cardboard flaps open. When I see the black guitar case, I freeze, and my mouth goes dry.

He didn't. *Oh, but he did.*

Like I'm opening a jewelry box containing diamonds the size of my fist, I flip the latches and lift the lid. My chest tightens as the breath I was holding whooshes out.

I reach down, almost afraid to trail my fingers along the pearlescent turquoise surface of the most beautiful guitar I've ever seen. With one fingertip, I trace the edge until I run up to the word *Gibson*. It's similar to the one I played at Rudy's the other night, but instead of black and bottom of the line, it's the top-of-the-line model and my favorite color, which Creighton couldn't have known.

As the iridescent flecks of paint glitter in the light, I can only picture how amazing it's going to look onstage.

I have to hear how she sounds, and instantly names start spinning in my head, because she has to have a name. Something feminine and kick-ass all at the same time. *Eliza Belle.* Okay, it's got a little country twang to it, but since that's what I'm going to be rocking out with on her, I think it's perfect.

I lift Eliza Belle out of her deep purple velvet-lined

case and hold her out in front of me. Perfection. Absolute perfection. *How did he know?*

My surprise rockets up a dozen more notches when I pull out the strap tucked in the case and take in the hand-tooled leather. My name is part of an intricate design of stars, guitars, and flowers. It's . . . I'm speechless.

Holy shit. I'm in trouble.

But I push that thought away to hook the strap on and carry Eliza Belle to the living room where my notebook rests on a side table. It's time to perfect some tunes.

All the while I'm strumming the chords, I'm thinking about Creighton and how I'm going to find the words to thank him for this gift.

CHAPTER
TWENTY-NINE

CREIGHTON

I open the door to my penthouse at six forty-five that night, and have the strangest urge to yell out something like *Honey, I'm home.* Although after yesterday, I now know there's no guarantee that Holly will *actually* be here, despite my threats.

She seems inclined to do whatever she likes, and that's something I'm going to have a hell of a time getting used to. When I give orders, I expect for them to be followed without question. But considering how much I enjoy punishing her for her lack of compliance, I suppose my complaints are not quite as intense as before.

But when it's her safety at issue, all bets are off. The idea of her walking around Manhattan by herself bothers me more than I would have ever imagined. She doesn't understand that she could easily be a target because of me.

Before I can say anything, though, the sound of Holly strumming the guitar and humming starts and then stops moments later.

I walk farther into the penthouse and see her sitting cross-legged in the middle of the couch, hunched over the guitar as she jots down something on the notebook in front of her. Her hair hangs loose over her shoulders, and she's wearing leggings and a gray long-sleeved shirt. Her feet are bare, and I think as long as I stay silent, she'll never realize I'm here.

I decide to watch her for a few minutes to test my theory.

My choice is rewarded when she starts again, closing her eyes as she plays a unique and unusually addictive tune. She doesn't sing, but her lips move, forming words that only she's aware of. In that moment, I want to see her in her element—onstage. My suspicion is that the confidence I see flashes of when she speaks so passionately about her career will shine even brighter when she's onstage. She's a unique creature, my wife.

She stops again and leans forward, scratching out something on the sheet and writing something new. When she glances up, she finally sees me standing in the doorway. Her eyes widen in surprise and she lays her pen down on the notebook.

"Hey, I didn't realize you were back."

"I was just watching you."

Her smile is quick and her face lights up. "It's not much yet, but it's going to be a hell of a song." Her head jerks toward the clock on the side table. "Oh crap, I didn't get ready. You wanted to leave at seven. I'll be quick. What do I need to wear? I kind of need some help in that area if you don't want me to embarrass you."

The easiness of her posture when she was playing is

gone, and I dislike that I'm ultimately the cause of it. I know my decision to ask Cannon for suggestions on what to do with Holly tonight was the right choice, because I want to give her that easiness back.

With honesty, I tell her, "You're fine the way you are. Grab your boots."

Holly's face is a picture of shock. "Are you screwing with me?" She glances down at what she's wearing. "Because I look like . . ."

"A sexy-as-fuck woman?"

"A girl from Kentucky."

"Which you are, so what's your point?"

"This is New York. I'm not New York chic. I already stand out enough; I don't need to stand out more."

"You're perfect. Grab your boots. We're going out."

CHAPTER THIRTY

HOLLY

Creighton is crazy. He wants to take me out like this? I trail after him into the bedroom and tug on my boots, watching as he changes out of his suit into some slacks and a button-down shirt that's marginally casual.

"I'm not going to be underdressed?" I ask. "Because you're looking a lot fancier than me."

He smirks. "Where we're going, you'll fit in better than I will. Trust me."

And once again, I have a decision to make. When he reaches the doorway I'm leaning against and holds out his hand, I make my choice.

"If you say so. Let's do this."

I tuck my hand into Creighton's and we leave the penthouse, but not until he heads back to the master suite to get me a coat, hat, and mittens, as well as a jacket for himself. I'm surprised by the gesture, but it makes more sense when I don't see a chauffeur-driven Bentley at the curb. Apparently we're walking.

Creighton leads me down the busy sidewalk, and we turn the corner onto an even busier street. People in New York truly never seem to settle in; they're always hurrying from here to there. I try to avoid looking like a tourist and staring up at the buildings, so I instead look at the people around me as we walk farther and finally turn again. We're heading toward a bank, and I'm completely confused.

"Where are we—?" I start to ask, but then I see a small black sign next to the bank.

Johnny Utah's.

"Right here," Creighton replies as he steers me toward the door beneath the small sign. "It might be the only one of its kind in Midtown, and a friend suggested we check it out."

We walk inside, and not only is the place already packed with the happy-hour crowd, there's a mechanical bull in the middle of a wrought-iron fenced-in circle, surrounded by thick pads.

I jerk my gaze up to Creighton's. "Really?"

"Yes."

"You gonna ride the bull?"

He smirks. "Are you?"

My own smile grows wide, and for the first time since I met him, I'm not ashamed of the accent I let color my words. "Baby, this ain't my first rodeo."

"Good girl. Because this I want to see."

We sidle up to the bar, and I slip my hat and mittens into my coat pockets as Creighton orders for both of us. I don't argue, especially because he's ordered two shots of whiskey. I'm reminded of our first night together at the

Rose Club, amazed at how different tonight is despite how little time has passed. It's crazy how everything can change so quickly.

"Only Prettier" by Miranda Lambert is playing on the bar speakers, and I have to smile. Her start wasn't all that different from mine, and look where she is now. She's also unashamedly herself. I could probably learn a thing or two from her.

But then again, she was married to a fellow country singer, like Tana, not a billionaire. This is a whole different situation. I'm trying to straddle two worlds, but at least for tonight, Creighton is making an effort to bring me to a world that isn't quite so foreign.

He slides one shot glass in front of me and raises his. "To us. We've officially outlasted at least one or two celebrity marriages. Britney Spears comes to mind."

I choke out a laugh before I can offer the toast back to him. "I can't even believe you know that."

"I think everyone knows about that." He continues holding up the shot glass and raises an eyebrow. "It's bad luck to not reciprocate. Toasts . . . and other things."

I smile, and it's genuine. This sense of humor isn't something I expected. "Well, I don't think we need any bad luck. So," I raise my glass, "to us."

As we clink glasses and toss the liquor back, my eyes burn, and it has nothing to do with the whiskey sliding down my throat. I'm just stunned by the fact that there is an *us*.

Me and Creighton Karas. My husband.

I squeeze my eyes shut and beat the sneaky tears back

before they can completely surface. Then I slap my shot glass down on the wooden bar.

"Let's do this." I jerk my head toward the mechanical bull.

A girl is riding it, her fancy black pencil skirt riding up and her suit jacket tossed to the side. Her boobs bounce against her tailored white dress shirt with each swivel and buck of the bull. She only makes it a few seconds before sliding off onto the mats. Apparently someone was ready for the workday to be over.

Now I'm gonna show them how a real country girl does it.

"We taking bets?" I ask Creighton.

"About how long you stay on, or how hard my cock is going to get watching you ride?"

My giggle breaks loose. "I don't need to take bets on your cock. We're getting pretty well acquainted, and I have a good feeling that he's going to like this a whole lot." I slide off the stool and slip my coat off my shoulders and toss it at him. "Let me show you how a country girl does it."

Creighton leans down, my coat in one hand, and whispers in my ear, "I know how this country girl does it, and she's got me hooked."

His words stun me into silence. It's the first indication he's given that he feels something for me beyond the need to possess me like his newest toy. I can't process this right now, in the middle of a bar, not with Montgomery Gentry and "Hillbilly Shoes" just starting to crank on the speakers. It's altogether too apt.

Creighton doesn't really know me. Not all of me. Not

the heart and soul of me that I pour into my songs. Not the indescribable high I get when I'm standing onstage. Not the tiny town where I'm the girl who made good, and yet I haven't been back. Not the important parts of me.

Will he still be hooked then?

I plaster a smile on my face to cover my racing thoughts. "I'll see you after I've made the eight," I say, and spin on my bootheel to walk toward the man at the edge of the bull pen.

CHAPTER
THIRTY-ONE

CREIGHTON

Holly makes the eight, and she looks like a goddess doing it.

I want to tear every man's eyes away from her, but even I'm too riveted by her smooth, graceful movements to do a damn thing but stare. It's not lurid like some of the other women who rode the bull before her—chest heaving and making a spectacle. Holly manages to look beautiful and sweet even in this.

When she climbs off and walks over, I'm waiting at the gate. My hand is out, and something surges inside me when she doesn't hesitate to close her fingers around it. She's learning to trust me, and that's not something even I can command. It's something that has to be offered freely, and she's starting to.

I'll take it. All of it.

I lean down and press a kiss to her forehead. Not only because it's my instinctual reaction, but because I want every man in this bar to be well aware that she's not available and never will be. Holly's mine.

I see. I want. I conquer. I keep.

"Your skills are outstanding," I say, slipping her coat back around her shoulders.

Her smile is triumphant. "At least there's one thing in this city I'm sure I can handle."

Keeping my head low, I reply, "I think there's more than one thing you've proven very competent at handling in this city." Her blush is already rising when I add, "Let's find our table."

Her eyes widen. "You want to eat here? Really?"

"Come on."

I lead her to the hostess stand and we're seated immediately, although I don't see any recognition on the hostess's face when she looks at me or Holly. As soon as we've put in an order for another round of drinks, Holly is staring down at her menu, lips pursed. She glances up at me, her eyes sparkling with humor.

"Do you ever roll up your sleeves a little, fancy man?"

"I've been known to."

"Good, because I'm ordering ribs, and there's no way I'll be able to eat them all, so you're gonna have to get your hands a little messy and help me out."

I reach out and unbutton one cuff and begin to roll it up before doing the same to the other. "You're not afraid of me, and probably one of the very few people who also isn't afraid to give me hell."

"How many people are on that list?" she asks, laughing as she reaches for the beer the waitress places in front of her.

I've told Holly next to nothing about my personal life,

and considering what I pushed her to share last night, I decide it's my turn.

"It's a short list, that's for sure. My sister would be at the top."

Holly chokes on her beer before setting it down and reaching for her napkin. "You have a sister?"

Her shock doesn't surprise me. "She's never in the papers, and I've made it clear that my personal life is as off-limits as I can make it. The only reason that works is because I own one of the three largest media companies on the planet."

Holly's confusion is evident. "So you control the flow of information about yourself? That seems like a dangerous power to have."

I shrug off her comment. "As much as I can, but there are plenty of others out there who won't bow to my dictates. You saw the headlines we made. That proves I don't have ultimate power."

"So back to your sister, what's her name, and is she older or younger?"

"Greer. She's younger by nine years. She's a first-year associate at a big law firm here in town. She's currently working her ass off while she could have a cushy job with me. But she's stubborn as hell, and won't come over to the dark side, as she calls it."

"First, her name is awesome, and second, doesn't being a lawyer in general make you part of the dark side? Who's really keeping track of that, right?"

I laugh, amused that she shares my skepticism of lawyers in general. "There is some truth to that.

Although I'm sure there are some decent ones out there. Maybe. Mine are sharks, so they don't count."

"So she's a smart girl, wants to make her mark without riding her big brother's coattails?" Holly asks.

"Yes, that's exactly it. But she can't change her last name, so she doesn't escape notice completely. Part of me thinks Greer requests the toughest projects with the shittiest hours just so she can prove herself. It would definitely be in line with her character."

"So she can make fun of you and not end up at the wrong end of that death stare of yours?"

"Death stare?" I tilt my head. "Is that what you call it?"

Holly nods, biting her lip. "You know the one; it says *stop talking or you'll regret it.*"

"Ah. That death stare." I know exactly what she's talking about. "It works, doesn't it?" I glare, or at least do my best to glare while I'm trying to keep from laughing. "Not anymore, it doesn't."

"We'll see about that. So other than little sis, who else?"

I have to actually think about the answer to this question, and the timing is right because our waitress returns for our order. As promised, Holly orders ribs, and I go for a steak. When the waitress leaves, I answer.

"That's pretty much it. Maybe Cannon, my EVP."

"What's an EVP?" Holly asks, reminding me that she's the one person in my life who doesn't speak corporate acronyms.

"Executive vice president. He oversees all of the division presidents, and keeps me from having to be involved in day-to-day bullshit unless it rises to a level of importance where I'm truly needed. It frees me up to deal with strategy and other things."

"Am I ever going to meet this Cannon guy?"

Cannon is one of the most important people in my life, and knows more about Holly than she'll likely ever know about him. If he didn't know I'd put out a hit on him, he'd probably try to steal her from me.

"That's very likely."

"Maybe I can meet him the next time I'm in town."

Holly's statement isn't all that subtle. She's checking to see if I forgot that she's leaving tomorrow.

What she doesn't realize is she's not the only one who's leaving. I'm not about to let my wife out of my sight for an extended period of time. It has nothing to do with trust, and everything to do with the fact that I'm not ready for her to be that far away from me.

"I'll have the jet ready to go tomorrow. I need to take care of a few things during the day, but I'll get you back to Nashville in time for dinner. It's a quick flight."

Her brow scrunches. "Does that mean you're going with me?"

"Did you expect me not to?"

She shrugs, and I wait a few moments before she finally speaks. "I don't know. I mean, you have your life and I have mine. I kind of figured we'd go to our separate corners and do what we need to do, and then regroup later."

Her plan is unacceptable on multiple levels. Any humor in my expression dies away.

"That's not happening. I'm not letting you out of my sight, let alone go to another state without me."

Dropping her gaze to her beer and the label she's now intent on peeling off, Holly is silent for a beat. "Okay, then."

"It'll be more than okay," I reply. "Just wait."

CHAPTER
THIRTY-TWO

HOLLY

"Just wait, he said. Just. Wait. I didn't realize he meant it so damn literally."

My words carry no heat or anger, just the heavy weight of disappointment. So much for Creighton and his big promises. I'd woken with a smile on my face this morning, remembering how much fun we'd had at the bar last night, but that smile had faded as the hours crept by today without a single word from Creighton. I've filled the time by working on my songs, but I thought he'd be back by now. Not only is he not back, he hasn't even called.

I look at the time on my phone again, and the text message that came in twenty minutes earlier from my manager.

CHANCE: *You back in Nashville yet? I need you here ASAP. Call me as soon as you're in town.*

I tap on my phone's browser and check the flight times to Nashville. If I leave now, I can get to JFK and be on a plane and back in Nashville by nine. A couple of hours later than the private jet that Creighton promised, but I have no choice.

Finally, I lose my temper. "Why won't he freaking answer me?" I yell at the room.

When he didn't show at four, I started to wonder. By four thirty, I couldn't stop myself from texting; he didn't reply. At five, I called; he didn't answer. It's five fifteen, and I decide to try one more time.

Before I can hit my contacts to bring his number up again, my phone vibrates with a text. I tense, heart leaping, but my hopes are crushed when I see Tana's name and not Creighton's.

TANA: *When are you getting in? I miss your face, and I want more dirty details.*

A wave of humiliation washes through me. You know what sucks worse than being forgotten by your husband at a very important moment? Having to admit it to your friends. It's one thing to know it yourself, but it's another to have to endure the pity that comes with making excuses for someone else when the person you're making excuses to can see right through you. I made excuses to people for my mama for years, and I swore I'd never put myself in that position again.

So that's one brilliant thing about text messages. You can ignore them until you're ready to reply.

Picking up my phone, I scroll through my contacts. Tapping on Creighton's mobile number, I hold my breath and cross my fingers . . . and it goes to voice mail.

Glancing at the clock, I see the deadline I set for him edging closer and closer. I pick the next number under

Creighton's name—his office. Shockingly, it's answered almost immediately.

"Karas International, this is Mr. Karas's line. May I help you?"

I pull myself together and say, "Is Mr. Karas available?"

The woman on the other end pauses. "May I tell him who is calling?"

"His wife."

Her pause is even longer this time. "Excuse me?"

"This is Holly Karas, and I'd like to speak to my husband." It's weird to say that name, but I guess it's mine.

"May I put you on hold, Mrs. . . . . Karas?"

"Yes, that's fine."

Generic music fills my ear, but it doesn't last long.

"Holly?"

It's not my husband's voice. I have no idea who it is.

"Yes, this is Holly."

"This is Cannon Freeman, I'm—"

"You're the EVP," I say, pulling the term from my memory, and he sounds surprised.

"Yes, that's right. I'm so sorry to tell you that Creighton is in the middle of something, and he can't step away. This is a pretty big deal, one our team has been working on around the clock—even when he was off having fun with you yesterday—and if he leaves the table right now, we'll lose too much ground. Is there something I can do for you?"

First the guilt comes, which I brush away. Creighton chose to take me out last night; it wasn't my decision. If he left his business in someone else's care, that was his choice. And then comes resentment laced with anger.

My business comes first. Creighton spoke those very words to me that first morning in Vegas. Then later, he promised not to do anything to put my career in jeopardy. Which is exactly what he's doing.

Well, guess what, Creighton? My business comes first for me, because it clearly doesn't come first for anyone else. Not you, not the record label, not anyone but me.

"There's nothing you can do for me, Mr. Freeman. No need to trouble him further."

I hang up the phone without giving him a chance to reply.

My phone buzzes again, and I think for a moment that it's Creighton's EVP calling me back.

It's not.

CHANCE: *Plans changed. We're on the road tonight. Get your ass here now. You miss this bus, and you're off the tour.*

Of course. I squeeze my eyes shut. *My husband is MIA, and I'm out of time.*

When it comes down to it, there's one lesson I've learned in my life: I have no one to count on but myself. It's sobering to realize I started to count on Creighton in this short period of time . . . and just shows how naive I truly am.

Thank you, Universe. I've learned my lesson.

I survey the penthouse apartment as I stand and head for the door. The credit cards with my married name on them sit on the counter, and all the clothes Creighton had delivered before I even agreed to his offer are hanging in the closet where they belong.

I've got my purse and my notebook and the clothes I wore on New Year's Eve. My pride dictates I take nothing that isn't mine to take. Even the beautiful guitar.

I'm worth more than the time it takes to make a phone call and have a personal shopper pick up something. I deserve a little common courtesy, especially when I've made it clear that there's one thing in my life that matters to me.

If what matters to me means nothing to Creighton, how can we ever make this work?

Instead of feeling like I matter to him even in the slightest, I'm once again relegated into afterthought status. I'm a convenience. A doll that's supposed to wait on the shelf for her turn to be taken down and played with when it's convenient for him, and obviously it's not convenient right now. He couldn't even take my damn phone call.

You know what? I deserve more than that.

"Good-bye, Creighton," I say to the empty room.

Holly and Creighton's story continues in *Dirty Pleasures* and *Dirty Together.*

You know you don't want to miss what's coming next! Visit https://meghanmarch.com/subscribe to sign up for my newsletter, and never miss another announcement about upcoming projects, new releases, sales, exclusive excerpts, and giveaways.

I'd love to hear what you thought about Holly and Creighton's story. If you have a few moments to leave a review, I'd be incredibly grateful. Send me a link at meghanmarchbooks@gmail.com, and I'll thank you with a personal note.

ACKNOWLEDGEMENTS

I've never written acknowledgments without a few tears falling, and honestly, I hope I never do. This is the first time I've written these thank-yous as a full-time author, and the feeling is utterly surreal. Like so many other writers, I crammed in my words whenever I could find a spare moment, between a day job and every other life commitment. Without the help of a village of people, I wouldn't be living this dream of being a full-time author, and my gratitude knows no bounds.

Special thanks go out to:

Dad, I miss you so much, but I know you're cheering on your little girl as I chase these big dreams. Thank you for teaching me not only to dream so big I scare myself most days, but for teaching me the power of hard work. There will never be a day that I don't count myself lucky to be your daughter.

Mom, you're the strongest woman I know, and I am in awe of your grace. I love you so much.

Pam Berehulke, editor extraordinaire, for once again helping me deliver the best story I'm capable of writing.

Chasity Jenkins-Patrick, kick-ass publicist, for talking me off more than one ledge and always pushing me in the right direction.

Natasha Gentile, for being a fabulous beta reader. Love your messages, lady!

The Meghan March Runaway Readers Facebook group, for being the most fabulous collection of ladies I've had the pleasure of (virtually) meeting. Hope to hug you all at events soon!

All the book bloggers who take the time to read and review this and any of my other books. Your time and dedication are truly appreciated.

My readers—I'm infinitely grateful that you've picked up this book. Without you, I wouldn't be living my dream.

ALSO BY MEGHAN MARCH

ABOUT THE AUTHOR

Making the jump from corporate lawyer to romance author was a leap of faith that *New York Times*, #1 *Wall Street Journal*, and *USA Today* bestselling author Meghan March will never regret. With over thirty titles published, she has sold millions of books in nearly a dozen languages to fellow romance-lovers around the world. A nomad at heart, she can currently be found in the woods of the Pacific Northwest, living her happily ever after with her real-life alpha hero.

She would love to hear from you.
Connect with her at:

www.meghanmarch.com

Made in United States
North Haven, CT
10 February 2024

48549579R00125